PIERS ANTHONY

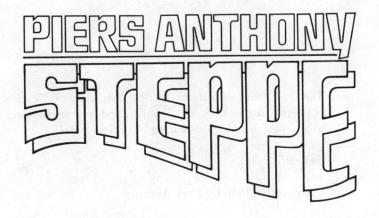

STEPPE

TOR

A TOM DOHERTY ASSOCIATES BOOK

STEPPE

Copyright © 1976 by Piers Anthony

A TOR Book

Published by Tom Doherty Associates
49 West 24 Street
New York, N.Y. 10010

Cover art by Boris Vallejo

First TOR printing: September 1985

ISBN: 0-312-93748-2

Printed in the United States of America

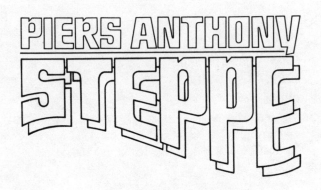

PIERS ANTHONY
STEPPE

Part One

UIGUR

Chapter 1

GORGE

Alp slapped Surefoot on the flank and guided him toward the gorge. The barbarians probably thought he would head for the open plain, but they were about to discover that civilization was not synonymous with stupidity. Not entirely!

He eased the pace as he picked up the cover of the scattered trees of a large oasis. Surefoot would need his strength for the gorge!

It would be better to stop here and rest—but Alp could not take the chance. Once the pursuers realized he was *not* rushing directly south in blind panic, they would cut back, killing any oasis peasants who failed to point the way. That would be in a matter of hours—no more.

He would not have had even that much leeway, had he arrived in time to fight for his wife and child. But their demise had saved him, for he had seen the enemy standards at his tent. Too many to fight . . .

He broke out of the protective hollow and climbed the ridge. There was treacherous country to negotiate, and he was hardly fool enough to rush it. If Surefoot sprained an ankle here—

Shapes raced out of the late afternoon sunlight on either side. Kirghiz! They had anticipated him after all!

Alp knew that retreat was impossible. The savages were almost within arrow range already, and their steeds were fresh. To flee was to be cut down from behind—much as his Uigur countrymen had been decimated.

His dry lips drew back over white teeth. There had not been time for a general alert against him. At least some of these riders had to be from the horde that had overrun Alp's estate. His discipline had stopped him from attacking suicidally then—but the current situation, though bad, was improved. He could make his first payment on a very large debt of revenge.

So he charged. Not for the diminishing open spot ahead, the center of the barbarian pincers, but for the left group of horsemen. There were four on that side—more than enough to do the job, but not so many that he couldn't take one or two with him as he went down. Perhaps three. They thought the Uigur had forgotten how to fight, that he had fled the massacre of his family because of cowardice . . .

The four Kirghiz rallied as he came at them, forming a half circle for him to enter. Their bows were ready, but with native cunning they held their fire until their target was sure.

Alp grinned again—the bared fangs of the wolf. They were right about the *average* Uigur, for his people had grown soft in the course of a century of dominance over the steppe country. Many had moved into the great city of Karabalgasun, high on the Orkhon River, forgetting their plains-riding heritage that had made these Turks great. The Khagan, ruler of the Uigur, had adopted the foreign religion Manichaeism, and the nobles had turned to scholarly pursuits. They had mastered the difficult art of writing, so as to record the legends and history of the world. Thus the Uigur's nomad power had waned while his intellectual power waxed—and thus the primitive Kirghiz on the northern reaches had been able to rebel and prevail. The enemy had sacked the capital city and brought ruin to the Uigur empire.

And desolation to Alp himself. Only the need to make his vengeance count as heavily as possible sustained him now. He was one of the few who had maintained the old skills while mastering the best of the new. He had no use for Manichaeism, so he had been out of favor with the Khagan. Only his resolute fighting posture had saved Alp from the wrath of his ruler. He had remained technically loyal, and the Khagan had needed sturdy warriors as officers, so an uneasy truce had prevailed.

Now all that was done, with the Khagan dead and his power obliterated. The Kirghiz intended to eliminate the most serious remaining threat to their newfound empire. And they had just about done it—they thought.

Alp's bow was in his hand, the first arrow nocked. He had designed the set himself: the bow was larger than normal and was braced by the finest horn available, with a gut string from the leading specialist. The arrows too were long and finely balanced. It had taken him years to settle on the ideal proportions for this weapon, and its elements had cost him much, but the superior instrument had been well worth it. He could shoot farther than any other man he knew, and with truer impact.

He fired, rising momentarily on his stirrups for better aim. The arrow made a high arc—and struck in the belly of the nearest Kirghiz. The man gave a horrible cry, quite satisfying to Alp, and dropped off his horse. "That for my son!" Alp muttered.

Immediately the other three fired—but one arrow fell short and two went wide. Alp's second was already in the air, and this time his aim was better. The point scored on the second barbarian's face, penetrating his brain. "That for my wife!"

Alp ducked down as Surefoot automatically responded to battle conditions and ran a jerky evasive pattern. The horse had been almost as difficult to obtain and train as it had been to design and make the bow—but again the effort had been worthwhile. Two more arrows missed—but at Alp's signal Surefoot reared and stumbled as if hit. The two remaining Kirghiz exclaimed with joy, seeing victory—and Alp's third arrow, fired from the side of his stumbling horse, thunked into the shoulder of one. The fool had sat stationary for an instant too long! "And that for me!"

Alp could take the fourth enemy easily—except for the five warriors of the other wing now closing in. Yet he could not afford to leave that man behind, free to take careful aim at the retreating target. Alp's bow was no advantage now, for he was well within the Kirghiz range, and there were no cowards or bad shots in the barbarian cavalry! The element of surprise was gone; the Kirghiz knew they faced a fighting nomad.

"Now that the amenities are over, we shall begin the fray," Alp said. "Uigur cunning against Kirghiz." He felt a bit better, for he had avenged his family for today. Tomorrow, if he lived, he would avenge it again—and so on, until the need diminished. Then he would seek another wife.

Alp touched Surefoot again in a special way, and the horse responded with the certainty of a reliable, well-loved friend. Surefoot leaped, landed, and tumbled, rolling all the way over before struggling to his feet. Alp's precious bow was flung wide.

The fourth Kirghiz clung to the side of his own mount, proffering no target, bow ready—waiting for the Uigur to show, dead or alive. But Surefoot rose and trotted on, riderless. The Kirghiz charged the place where the horse had rolled, expecting to dispatch the injured rider—and died as Alp's accurately thrown knife caught his throat.

Surefoot charged back. Alp fetched his bow and leaped aboard. *Now* he fled—and the five other riders were still beyond range.

Alp knew he was not out of it yet. The Kirghiz would surely gain as Surefoot tired, and all Alp's tricks would be futile the next time around. The savages were very quick to catch on to new combat techniques and very slow to forgive them. If he exhausted his horse by racing to the gorge . . .

13

He looked behind and saw the five pressing on deter-
minedly, not even pausing to aid their fallen. He had no
choice.

The gorge was a long crack in the earth and rock. It had
been created, the legends said, by the kick of an angry jinn
generations ago. Its shadowed depth was filled partway with
rubble and the bones of enemies thrown there. The gorge
extended for many hours' ride—but most men spent those
hours rather than risk the certain death of a fall into its
narrowing crevice.

A good horse could leap it, though. If properly trained and
guided. And fresh.

Surefoot was not fresh. He had barely held his lead over
the five Kirghiz and sweat streamed along his sides. The
enemy would be within arrow range the moment Alp slowed
or turned.

There was still no choice. If he crossed the gorge, he
would be safe to pursue his vengeance at his leisure. The
barbarians' untrained steeds would balk, or fall short. If any
did hurdle it, Alp could pick them off singly as they landed.
That would be an easy start on tomorrow's tally!

By the time the rest circled around the crack, he would
long since be lost in the countryside.

But first he had to hurdle it.

He urged Surefoot forward as the rift came into view. The
mighty horse knew what to do. He was hot and tired, but he
did not balk or falter. He leaped into the air.

Not far enough. The hard run had sapped too much of his

14

strength, cutting down his speed at the critical moment. His front hooves landed firmly, but his rear ones missed. For a moment they scrambled at the brink; then horse and rider tumbled backwards into the chasm.

Who will avenge Surefoot? Alp thought wildly.

Chapter 2 ─────────────

HELL

Alp knew instantly that it was not heaven, for his horse was not with him. Alp was uncertain of his own disposition in death, but Surefoot was heaven-bound: of that there could be no doubt.

Therefore Alp was in the hell of the chasm. That was the worst possible outcome—but at least he had the dubious advantage of recognizing it. In life he had prospered by his wits as much as his strength; in death it should not be otherwise. He need have no scruples in dealing with the demons he found here, whatever their aspect.

Their aspect was strange indeed! They wore costumes roughly resembling his own, but their tunics were not of true linen and their helmets were obviously unserviceable for combat. Which meant, again, that these were demons, mock-men, whose dress was mere pretense and whose purpose was devious.

Alp himself was naked now. Worse, he was weaponless. His bow, sword and dagger were gone, and no quiver of arrows clung to his back. Naturally the demons were giving him no chance to fight them. The average demon was a coward, skulking in shadows, seldom showing his ugly face in man's land.

One came toward him, carrying a helmet. The headpiece was far too cumbersome for practical use, being so broad and deep that it would fall almost to a man's shoulders, blinding him. Alp shied away, baring his teeth in an effort to frighten the thin-faced demon away.

This was effective, for the creature paused and backed off, though he was taller than Alp, true to his ilk.

Another demon moved, placing a hand in a box of some sort. Alp watched him covertly, in case he should be fetching a knife. But the thing only touched a round knob.

Coincidentally, Alp's power of motion left him.

Magic! He should have expected that, though there seemed to be no way to avoid it. He had hardly believed in magic when alive, knowing most shamans to be charlatans. Of course he had *professed* belief so as to stay clear of unnecessary complications. But this was death, and different laws prevailed. These creatures might be laughable as physical fighters, but in their own black arts they were matchless.

It was a necessary reminder that no entity could safely be held in contempt. The Kirghiz were too dull to master literacy, yet were formidable warriors. The demons could not compete with Alp physically but possessed the skills of another realm. If he hoped to survive this state, he would have to make a special effort to understand its laws.

The first demon, seeing Alp immobilized by the spell, now screwed up his courage and set the gross helmet over his head. Alp's sight was blotted out. He strove to break free but could not move. Still, he was not suffocated; evidently the demon did not realize that the prisoner's head was the wrong shape for such torture.

Actually, suffocation would be one way to escape this region. If he died here, he would proceed to the next level of the afterlife, never to return. Perhaps his fortune would be better, there.

No—it was not in the Uigur to surrender! Better to fight for *this* life—which might not be a bad one, once he escaped these demons. Perhaps this was no more than the initiation test: only the capable visitor managed to remain.

Something strange was happening. It developed slowly, like the barely perceptible rising of the sun at dawn—but like the sun, it spread its influence pervasively. Alp began to understand things about these demons.

They did not consider themselves demons. In their own odd language they were "Galactics"—human beings from far away, representatives of a mighty empire than spanned a much greater region than did the Uigur realm at its height. That empire extended over planets and systems and constellations—though these were concepts of such sorcerous complexity and incongruity as to baffle his mind. He knew them to be pretense and illusion nevertheless—because demons were things of the fundament, not the welkin. Soil-grubbers, not sky-flyers. So that much he could set aside as irrelevant.

Or could he? Again he had to remind himself that the rules of his own realm did not necessarily apply. Conceivably demons *did* master heaven, here—or thought they did.

The demons spoke a language of their own. Not Uigur, not even Chinese. Their speech had no writing. They had "machines" to do their bidding, these devices being jinn-like entities housed in metal, capable of phenomenal wizardry.

The demons were engaged in a war that was not a war but a game, in which those killed did not really die yet could not exactly return. Reincarnation was the only possibility—but for this they had to pay a fee.

It was too much! Alp closed his mind to this madness—but found there was no escape from it. The helmet was not a suffocation device after all; its torture was more subtle. It crammed unacceptable information into his shuddering brain, destroying his comfortable patterns of belief.

The helmet claimed it was actually a force-education device that was radiating demon-information into his head like a shower of arrows. True torture of hell!

Finally they took the thing off, but Alp remained frozen in place. Had the spell not been on him, he would have fallen to the floor.

"He should comprehend now," one demon said. "Though you never can tell, with an actual barbarian."

So it was like that, Alp thought grimly. The Kirghiz had figured him for a soft civilized fool, and these Galactic-demons figured him for a stupid primitive.

"Release the stasis," another said. "We can't interrogate him this way."

So they meant to question him—and could not release his

jaw without nullifying the entire spell. Already he was grasping the limits of their magic!

A touch of the box—and the spell was broken. So that was the instrument: a machine! Alp was free—completely. He verified this by flexing muscles that did not show: calves, buttocks, back of the neck. All in order.

But he put his hand slowly to his head as if dazed. When he acted, that magic box would be a prime target!

A Galactic stepped toward him, an ingratiating smile on his shaven face. "Salutations, warrior."

Alp returned the creature's gaze dully. Demons were always fairest of speech when they intended mischief! He grunted.

"I knew it!" one of the others said. "Stupid. Can't orient."

"Terrified, more likely," another said. "Primitives are normally superstitious, afraid of sorcery. All his life on the plains he never experienced anything like this in his narrow existence. Give him a chance. We've invested heavily to fetch him here."

"Understatement of the century!" the third muttered. "A time-snatch of a millennia and a half—we'll all be broke if this doesn't pan out!"

"I'm in debt already," the last muttered.

A millennia and a half, Alp thought. Millennium, correctly; the demon usage did not precisely match the helmet language. Significant? In his terms, at any rate, fifteen hundred years, or thirty lifetimes. But time stretched two ways. Was it the period before man had arisen on the plains, or after man had passed?

"Speak, warrior," the demon in front said. "We wish to

21

know about you and your society.'' There was that in his manner that suggested insincerity. The language of facial expression and bodily posture transcended man-demon distinctions.

"Uhg,'' Alp said, still feigning ignorance. They didn't want to know about him nearly as badly as he wanted to know about *them*! Obviously they were not omniscient, and they also thought they could lie to him, which meant they could be fooled themselves. What did they really want?

"All for nothing!'' the first of the three demons said. "We gambled our entire Game fortunes on this ridiculous snatch from the past—and fetched a moron!''

The leader refused to give up. "You are from a great culture, warrior. We are your friends. Tell us who your leader was—*is*. Your king.''

So the creature wanted information about the Uigur empire—not knowing that it had fallen or that the Khagan had been slain. Obviously the magic helmet could not extract information the same way it projected it. These were political spies of some sort who had an interest in worldly power. Why?

And the one behind had verified that Alp was from the demons' past—making these entities of the time after the downfall of man. They should know, therefore, the full history of the steppe region and have no need to ask him. Another indication that they were concealing the whole truth. This was no more and no less than he had expected from demons, whose nature did not change from year to year and whose purposes seldom aligned with those of true men.

The leader shrugged. "He won't respond. I suppose we had better return him to stasis while we consider—''

The Galactic nearest the spell-box reached toward it.

Alp launched himself, knowing he could wait no longer. He clubbed the leader-demon with the hardened side of his hand in passing, knocking it back, and dived for the box.

He was too late. The other demon's hand was already on it, turning the knob. Alp's body went dead.

But momentum carried him forward. He crashed into the box and the demon behind it. Both toppled over. There was a startled cry, a crackling sound, a moment of intense pain— and Alp was free again.

He saw a curtained window—but the remaining two Galactics stood between him and it. Alp had no bow, no arrows and no blade. He charged them anyway, kicking at one while butting the other. Then he leaped through the aperture.

Alp had not really expected to discover the plains of his homeland outside, for he knew the land of demons differed from mortal geography. In one region there was a magnetic mountain that snatched all metal away from men who rode by; in another the sun shone brightly at midnight. So he was prepared for something unusual here.

Still, he was amazed. The curtain was not physical, neither of wool nor horsehide; rather it was a tingling surface like that of a chill river. The notion of taking a bath was dismaying! And beyond this barrier were no trees, *ger* or desert sands, but a complex canyon of many colors.

It had to be the nether region of the gorge he had fallen into, though he had never imagined it could be so vast and splendid! Bright boulders rolled along narrow channels, and lights rose and fell *inside* the opposite canyon wall.

No—his new understanding told him that the boulders

were cars—wheel-less wagons able to roll uphill without being hauled by horses. The lights were in antigravity elevator shafts: magic hoists that carried men up and down without weight. Demon tricks, of course, called "science." He had no inherent fear of it, but he realized that he should treat it with extreme caution. A living demon killed men for the mere joy of it, but magic science acted without joy or sorrow.

Alp was naked, weaponless, and horseless. Was Surefoot here? He saw no bones. And of course he had already decided that his mount would not be here in hell, not even in the hell for horses. That was the nature of *man's* hell: to be without horse and weapon.

His appraisal of the canyon had taken only an instant, but already the scuffling sounds in the chamber behind made it clear that the Galactics were coming after him. That was the system of hell too: perpetual pursuit, and torture upon capture. But now he knew that not all demons had the same specific objectives; most likely the other demons of this realm had other warriors to torment and would ignore him. If he could kill the four assigned to him, as he had killed the four Kirghiz, he would have no quarrel with those outside.

Kill? Not precisely. His Galactics were associated with the Game, and in that context the act of killing did not accomplish the usual relegation to an afterworld. There were strange things about this Game—but he didn't have time to work it out now, though it was all in his helmet-sponsored memory. He had to move.

He ran down the channel he found himself on. Above it were other channels, and below it were more, like ropes stretched the length of the canyon. This was a street in a city—neither road nor town like any he had known in life. Karabalgasun was a city, and it had streets, but the houses were not tall and the roads were flat on the ground. The cities of the far places he had read about were similar: Changan in China, the Middle Kingdom; Babylon in the southwest.

Now he realized that the path itself was moving! He had stepped onto a woven mat being dragged along, and it was carrying him along with it, as though he rode the back of a monster serpent.

As he moved, the other demons on the pathway began to take notice of him. He would have observed them sooner had he not been distracted by the awesome depths of the canyon opening below him as he moved out. There was no bottom to it!

The females—dainty of limb, thin of face and fair of complexion—for demons—averted their eyes modestly. The males scowled. Nakedness was a taboo here, he realized—or a mark of subservience. That was why he had been stripped. Hell overlooked no torture! He had to get clothing, so that he could conceal his status and pass among the demons un- recognized.

"Hey, you!" one of them called in the demon-tongue, Galactic. It was a guard, a police official.

Alp saw that the creature was armed, so he stopped. He stepped into an alcove on the side, to get off the moving belt. They did not use swords here, or bows, or even daggers, but they had effective magic weapons nonetheless. Most effec- tive! He would have to plumb his new knowledge for details, because he was already aware that the fighting instruments he had known would be almost useless in this situation.

25

"What stunt is this?" the guard demanded. "You drunk or crazy?"

Alp knew he would have to make his first speech in the new language. His own Uigur vocabulary would instantly give him away. This demon was neither friend nor enemy, but an officer of law charged with maintaining order in hell. His question was rhetorical, as there was no alcohol or insanity in this framework. A proper answer might actually place the guard on Alp's side.

"I—suffered an accident," Alp said haltingly. "I fell—and woke without clothing. I do not know exactly where I am or how to return home."

The police guard squinted at him. "Put out your hand."

Alp did so. The demon slapped a disk against his palm. Its nature was not clear; this was the first tangible gap in the helmet knowledge. Had a swift arrow of information missed his head?

"That's the truth, but not the whole truth," the guard said, looking at the disk. "Care to try again?"

A magic truth disk! Now Alp understood. The information was in his mind after all, but he had not recognized the concept. How fortunate he had not attempted an outright lie!

Actually, it would not be proper to lie to any of these demons other than the four he fled from, for the others were not his enemies. He could not condemn them all merely because they had the misfortune to be demons. Technically, he was now a demon himself!

"I am an Uigur subchief. My family was killed by barbarians. I obtained vengeance but died while escaping the Kirghiz, and now I am in hell without horse, weapons or dress."

Actually the words he used were not precisely analogous to the concepts of his people, but more than a language barrier was involved. This language of Galactic seemed to have a plethora of terms relating to vehicles and ships, but almost none relating to important Uigur matters such as "stirrup," "bowstring" or "gorge." "I escaped the four demons assigned to torture me—and there they are!" he pointed.

The guard's round eyes widened. "That *is* the truth, as you see it—but there's little sign of derangement! Mister, you've been hyped! I'll nail them all!"

The demons saw the guard and tried to retreat, but he whipped out a portable stunner. Docilely they coasted down to line up beside Alp.

"Officer," the leader said respectfully through his obvious discomfort. "We're in Steppe. We were interrogating this man when he attacked us and plunged into the street."

"Steppe!" the guard exclaimed, grimacing beautifully. "I should have known. What in hell are you clowns doing on this level?"

So the demons admitted this was hell!

"Our equipment is here. We had no intention of coming into the street, but we couldn't let the primitive run loose—"

Alp kept silent. He was learning a great deal of value, more by the memories evoked by the dialogue than by the actual words. His new memory had to be drawn out in comprehensible segments to be useful. "Steppe" was not a land but a synonym for the Game—a game of life and half-death. A game that somehow involved Alp himself.

"He claims you kidnapped him," the guard retorted. "Game or no Game—"

"No, officer! We pooled our resources and fetched him from the past. He's a native of the real Steppe. We mean to interrogate him and ship him back—"

Back! Alp's face remained passive, for there was no sense in letting them know how well he comprehended. Back to life, and to vengeance among the Kirghiz—

No! This was *not* death, but a removal to another age of man. Back meant true death for him and true hell! Better to fight it out right here; if he won, he had new life, and if he lost, he would be no worse off than he had originally thought.

Chapter 3

HIDING

The guard checked the demon-leader's story with his truth-disk. Actually there was no sense in thinking of them as demons anymore; they were in fact men, like him. "Very well," the official said. "Get him off the street—and see that you don't intrude on this level again, or I'll run you in! I know you're violating Game regulations."

"We appreciate it, officer!" the man said. "Now—"

Alp moved with a speed and certainty unfettered by either clothing or Galactic scruples. He snatched the stunner from the officer's holster, aimed it the way he had seen it aimed, and pressed the visible stud.

There was a snap. All five men stiffened and toppled as the invisible beam mowed them down. They fell across the moving belt and were carried away.

Alp lowered the weapon, for which he was developing

hearty respect—and his right leg went numb. The device was still operating! He stumbled, balancing on his left leg while he fiddled with the stud. It snapped up, stopping the force— but his leg remained dead.

Other Galactics were coming toward him. Alp held the stunner well out of the way and ran awkwardly, clinging to the beltway rail for support. There was no pain in his stunned leg and no visible injury, but it would neither respond to his will nor support his weight. It had become a useless attachment that tended to drag.

He had to get out of sight! He put the stunner between his teeth, heaved himself over the rail and climbed down outside the belt channel, using both hands and his good foot.

There was a framework under the belt, buttressed by a pattern of beams. Alp clung to these, looking for a way down. He was in good physical shape, like any true Uigur, but climbing and hanging were not his forte.

There was no descent. The gorge reached down sickeningly, making a drop unthinkable, and the belt support stretched twenty meters in either direction before meeting vertical supports.

Alp was a horseman, not a bird. But there was no horse, and his leg still lacked sensation. He proceeded along the beams, passing from one to the next, hand across hand.

Now people on the belts below were looking up. He *still* wasn't hiding very well! He had to get away from here and get some clothes—before more policemen converged.

His arms were fast tiring. Alp hauled himself back up the side and fell over the rail with the last of his strength. He had been using his muscle instead of his brain, and that was bad.

The five stunned bodies had been carried away. He knew they had not recovered yet because his leg had not—assuming the effect of the beam was reversible. A lone man was riding the belt toward him. And in the sky, above the highest to the criss-crossing beltways, Alp saw a flying shape like a monstrous mosquito, its wings invisible. A hovercraft, his new memory said. More antigravity—an opaque concept.

He took the stunner from his mouth, aimed it at the lone man, and pressed the stud. The man fell forward, and Alp caught him. His leg gave way and they both collapsed. Alp made sure the stud had not locked down this time, so as not to deaden any more of his own anatomy, then turned his attention to the man.

He was narrow-faced, like most of the Galactics, and had the same burned-off hair style Alp had noted passingly on the men of the lower beltways. The four demons had approximated Uigur style tonsure, with the main mass braided and thrown back from the forehead; but it seemed other Galactics declined to maintain tresses of appropriate length.

Quickly he yanked off the man's tunic. The Galactic's bared skin was paler than Alp's own, and more hairy; the muscles were comparatively flabby, and there was some fat. Could this be a noble? Certainly the body was that of neither peasant nor horseman!

Alp put the tunic over his own head. The material was like quality silk, light but strong. There was also underclothing; Alp had neither time nor inclination to don it himself, but he did get it off the other. The man's genitals were unusually large: yes, surely a noble!

But an enemy noble, or at least not a friend. Alp let the

man ride on down the belt, while he leaned against the stationary rail of the alcove. He was just beginning to fight with his brain.

The insect in the sky expanded into a floating machine. A police craft. Alp had suspected it, for his new awareness told him that only officials and police were permitted the use of hovercraft within the city proper. That was why he had acted so rapidly. But now he waited.

The craft approached the belt. The machine was hollow like a gourd, and two more guards were inside. One opened a hatch and jumped out on the belt. "There he is!" he cried. "Naked man!"

The policeman caught up with the body and hauled it to an alcove, using a small magic rug to make it float. The vehicle came alongside, and the two men passed the unconscious one inside. Still Alp did not move.

The craft departed, moving upward with no wings. At last Alp smiled. He had feared the ruse would not be successful, and that he would have to stun these police too—if it were possible to affect the one in the craft. Had they suspected his identity they could have stunned him without warning, finishing his fling at freedom. That was the gamble he had taken, not from boldness but necessity. It had worked—and almost too easily.

But now he had to secure his position in this world. He needed better clothing, and money or barter, and a horse—or at least a moving machine. And a suitable territory to roam. For these Galactics could not be stupid; he had fooled them once, but like the Kirghiz they would be on guard the next time. Their magical resources were far greater than his.

First, his hair. He possessed no knife to cut it short, so he would have to do it the hard way. He sat down so as to free both hands, taking a pinch of hair between his fingers with his left hand and a section of that with his right. He yanked. A tuft came loose, hurting his scalp despite his protective grip.

Alp laid the black strand down and quickly unbraided the remainder. Then, yank by yank, he dismembered his fine ebony mane, leaving a ragged pasture where there had been Uigur pride. Another torture of hell—and he had to do this to himself!

Sensation was finally returning to his leg. That meant the others he had stunned would be coming to. There would soon be a second alarm.

He placed the mat of hair in an inner pocket of the tunic; hair could be fashioned into rope when required. He hoped no blood showed on his head; his hasty barbering had been brutal in places.

Alp rode down the belt until he came to a crossbelt. He took that, then found a descending lift and rode that. The feel of weightlessness alarmed him, but he quelled his stomach. He felt more secure nearer the ground. While he traveled he used his brain some more, digesting his new information and seeking ways to use it.

This was a remarkable land. There were no true horses and few plains. There were more people here than in all of populous China. Machines did almost everything—even thinking and copulating. Men could still do these things, but the machines did them better. A machine could spawn a human baby if properly primed; this was called "hydroponic insemi-

33

nation" or something similar. Appalling—but so it had been for generations. And the stars in the sky were no longer specks of light on the dome of the night, but bright suns— and near many of these suns were other worlds like this one.

People were numbered. Machines provided their food. A man was limited not by the strength of his arm and the accuracy of his bow, but by the amount of intangible wealth he possessed, reckoned in points. Naturally this made for extreme laziness. The Chinese were soft, while the hard-riding Uigurs were hard—or had been, before civilization had softened them and made them vulnerable to the Kirghiz. But among these Galactics the edge of war no longer necessarily gave the hard men the advantage; the machine weapons and magic were far too strong. So there was no natural halt to the process of decay—some year the machines themselves, like the Kirghiz, would rebel and take over. Alp well understood the process!

Meanwhile, there was the Game. The competitive nature of the minority of Galactics was sublimated there. The conditions of times past were duplicated—crudely—and history was re-enacted—approximately. A man's fortune and reputation in the galaxy was determined largely by his performance in this Game, and the most ambitious men participated. Even women! In the Game was all the action and lust and intrigue that the mundane galaxy lacked.

It took only a minute's thought to show Alp that he would be far more at home in the Game than in the "real" galaxy, for that mundane scheme was as foreign as hell to him, literally, while the Game—

The Game was Steppe. Uigur and Chinese dominated it.

Its present stage in history was about the year 830, Christian Era. Alp cared not one sheep-dropping for Christianity, but he was satisfied to orient on its time scale for now.

Alp himself had been snatched from a time about ten years later—841. That was why the four demons—actually Game players—had used their machine to fetch him from the canyon just before he died at the bottom. His absence made no difference to his world, for he was dead there anyway. A complex concept of "paradox" governed that. The four players had hoped to draw information from him concerning the intervening years he had experienced—the years between 830 and 841. Information that would profit them enormously in the Game.

This was important, he realized, for they had gone to a great deal of trouble for the sake of learning about those years. Why? Why should news of a decade matter that much? What good could it actually do them? Particularly when they could look it up in a history text?

No, they could *not* look it up, for these Galactics were illiterate! Their machines did all their reading for them, turning it into pictures on windowlike screens. They knew only what their machines told them.

And—the four demons did not know precisely *when* Alp was from! They had fetched him from their past, but they had had to take only the man whose removal could not affect their own history. So they had oriented on the bottom of the canyon, waiting for someone to fall—and few men *did* fall, alive, because it was in Uigur territory and Uigurs were not fools about canyons. Only the pressure of the chase had forced Alp himself to attempt that leap when unprepared.

Probably he was the only man to die that way in twenty years—and possibly much longer. So the players might have wanted a man fifty years beyond Game-time—and had to settle for Alp. He was actually worth less to them than they supposed.

Yet surely they could ask the machines for what they wanted to know! That seemed easier than delving all the way into the past. The knowledge-machines still obeyed men.

No, they did *not!* Certain areas of knowledge were blanked from public awareness. This history of the steppe-country of Asia; of the Vikings of Europe; of the Moslem Arabs, the pre-Columbian Amerinds, and pre-European Africans. What these histories entailed Alp did not know, for the other names were unfamiliar to him. Those adventures could hardly rival the activities of the steppe, regardless!

But he understood the principle: for some reason the machines had been set not to give out these histories, thus keeping the Galactics ignorant. There were many such gaps in the record, his helmet-education informed him; some histories had been taught fifty or sixty years ago but not, since.

One gap was only partial: Steppe. Because Alp had studied the history of his own people, from Turk to Kao-Kiu to Tolach to Uigur—first a minor subtribe, then an increasingly powerful nation of nomads, and finally masters of all the steppe, equals of the civilized Chinese. Alp knew a thousand years of local events in fair detail. Surely there was more in the machines, following his own time—but that of course was blank to him.

Why was this historical ignorance fostered? To understand that, he had first to understand the nature of the Game.

Then it came clear, and he knew what he had to do.

Chapter 4

GAME

The beltways and lifts did not extend into the upper-most reaches. Alp had to take an internal elevator—and there trouble struck.

An alarm sounded as he entered.

Alp leaped back before the closing doors trapped him. He had not had experience with alarms before, but he had a lifetime's experience with mischief. His reflexes seldom betrayed him.

Now he remembered: key transports were equipped with personnel scanners. And all human clothing carried identification codes. He had plucked out much of his hair uselessly, missing what was there in his new memory to see. Obviously the police had discovered their error and put out a bulletin for the clothing of the robbed citizen. The chase was on again!

If he continued to wear this tunic, he would quickly be run down, now that they had a fix on him. Their magic machines could sniff out an identity unerringly; better to have an angry jinn on his trail! But if he removed the tunic, he would be a naked man again—another sure mark. Either way, capture and death—because he was not a proper citizen of this universe.

But he had only a little farther to go! Once he reached the Game, he would have more than a fighting chance.

He ripped off his tunic and dropped it off the edge of the beltway, saving only his handful of hair. The cloth fluttered down, carrying the telltale identity with it. Of course the police could identify human bodies too—but another complex principle called "personal privacy" made that difficult. A body had to be taken to the police station, where the number on it could be brought out by the special equipment there, for recognition to be certain. Even then, there had to be special authorization before the information could be circulated. The typical Uigur Khagan would never have tolerated such restrictions!

Alp himself had no Galactic number—but since he would be the only living man without one, they could readily identify him. He did not know whether the alarms were set to respond to the absence of any number; but in any event, his nakedness betrayed him.

He still had the stunner. He flicked it on and off at the next man he encountered. The citizen stiffened and would have fallen had Alp not caught him. This one was small and frail.

Alp hauled the tunic over the Galactic's head—and discovered the body beneath was feminine. He had been about to don this new apparel, knowing it would take the police a while to catch up with the changed number, but now altered his plan. There seemed to be no difference between man-tunics and woman-tunics, but no self-respecting warrior would wear female apparel!

This was the first Galactic woman he had seen up close. Her hair was burned short and her body was slender, but otherwise she was in no way inferior to the standards he knew. Why had she dressed like a man? Or were the men dressing like women? Had the long-haired citizens he had seen below actually been women, or—his new memory pro-vided the term—transvestites? It was a sorry world when women pretended to man's status—and got away with it!

But that was the way it was today, he realized. There were no requirements for the sexes. Some men preferred to be overtly masculine, and some women splendidly feminine; but the majority fell into a sexless anonymity. An anonymity he had emulated by reducing his hair; there would have been nothing wrong with his warrior's braid! Every citizen's right to individuality was respected—and also his freedom *from* individuality. At least, this was so in public.

Alp dropped the tunic off the belt. Then he stripped away the woman's underclothing and dropped it over also. As the woman moved, regaining consciousness (because he had dosed her with the shortest possible stun), he propped her against the moving rail and let her travel on, naked.

Nudity: there was a major taboo showing up all the Galac-tics' freedom of individuality as specious. Alp, sensibly, would rather go naked than wear a woman's tunic; these foolish people would rather exchange sexes than show their bodies. Of course, if Alp's own body were as flabby as what he had seen here, he might conceal it too . . .

Another citizen arrived, male, and Alp treated him the same way. Then two more came together. This was more difficult, but he managed. Then another woman, similarly processed. A line of people was moving down the belt.

Now the earlier cases realized their condition. Horrified, they fled to other belts and other levels, trying desperately to avoid contact with other people. It was a hilarious game of hide and seek. The sphere of nudity was expanding!

A police craft appeared. Alp rode down the belt himself, gesticulating as if in dire embarrassment. He was one of several—and the policeman could not distinguish him from the others!

Alp jumped into another elevator. This time no alarm rang. Good! He made it to the highest level and charged forth as though crazed.

But more police craft had assembled. Evidently they were taking no chances and were rounding up all the naked citizens. One flying machine oriented on Alp, gaining on him.

Alp dived for a special booth marked GAME ENTRY. "Sanctuary!" he cried as the police came up.

The door slid closed, and the clamor outside abated. "Identity?" a neutral voice inquired in Galactic.

"Anonymous," Alp said. He had rehearsed this dialogue in his mind during the chase.

"Entry fee?"

"Advance credit."

"Advance credit is not granted on an anonymous basis."

This was the crux. "I plead an exception. I am not a Galactic citizen."

"Your hand."

Alp held out his hand. Something touched it. "Intriguing," the voice of the Game Machine said. He knew it was the Machine, because there was now a superior quality about it, indicating intelligence. He knew the Machine would have the truth from him—if it so desired. He was at its mercy.

He also knew that machines did not care about human concerns. He was gambling that its disinterest in whether he lived or died was matched by its disinterest in the need of the police to capture him. The Game Machine could learn the truth about him—and not bother to give it away.

But it probed no further. "What indication is there that prospective winnings will be sufficient to repay such advance credit?"

"Technical expertise." The words came with difficulty, for both language and concepts were foreign. What he was really saying was that he would be a skilled player.

Now the police were peering in the transparent aperture, but they could not intrude until the Machine ejected him. He had to convince it to accept him into the Game!

"Of what nature?"

"Extrapolation of events." That meant he would be a lucky guesser. He could not claim to know the immediate future of Steppe—the past ten years of his own life—for then the Machine might suspect he had snooped on the program.

"One technical question."

"Agreed." As if he could refuse! This was another point of decision. If he could convince it that he was a good risk despite his anonymity, it would stake him to the minimum entrance fee of one hundred points. If not—

"What is the likely fortune of Wu-Kiai?"

Alp's hopes collapsed. "I do not know that name."

"Perhaps you know him as Uga."

Alp thought. "I do know of a chief by that name. A Uigur; a strong, violent man." He considered carefully. Actually he knew Uga very well, for that man had also been out of favor with the Khagan and had assumed much greater power when the Khagan died. But supposedly Alp was extrapolating, and he had to be cautious. "I believe he will rise high—but he lacks the judgment to be a really effective leader. No doubt he will die in battle."

"Here is a sampling of available parts. Make your selection."

Alp's pulse leaped. "You are extending credit?"

"That depends on your selection."

The Machine was candid! But Alp was half there.

A picture-screen illuminated. As the voice named each man, an image showed. This was followed by a brief description: current family and position and personality. The summary was fair; Alp had known several of these men personally. Obviously the Machine had done thorough research.

Could Alp himself be in the Game records? There was a nervous twitch down his back. At this historical date he would be but a stripling, as yet not come into his demesnes, as yet unmarried. But later he would be a chief . . . and perish in the gorge. An inferior part!

Credit was never extended for more than the minimum, which meant he could not obtain a really promising part. The quality of the part offered depended on the amount of the entry fee paid. Yet even the least likely prospect could turn out to be a winner; that was part of the appeal of the Game.

Alp knew that more than one of these prospects had died in the decade following the present Game-time of 831. Naturally the Machine knew this, but the players did not. If Alp chose wrongly, he would "die"—actually, be ejected from the Game—very soon, with no chance to succeed in the manner that would earn him back his entrance stake. Such figurative death would soon become literal, for him, since the police would be waiting outside.

"These are all Uigur," Alp said.

"Those are the most commonly desired parts at the moment," the Machine said. "There are many others. What group do you prefer?"

"Kirghiz." Alp was disgusted, having to consider a barbarian part, but he needed quick success.

"An interesting choice." Kirghiz parts appeared on the screen.

Was the Machine suspicious? It could not really find anything "intriguing" or "interesting," for it had no emotion. Such words could be signals of trouble. It had to know that the Kirghiz were about to supplant the Uigur in Steppe. But there was scant indication of this ten years before the actual overthrow.

"No, they are too barbaric," Alp said. "No future there. A Uigur is best, after all."

"As you wish." The Machine was giving away no hint!

Alp chose a literate Uigur subchief named Ko-lo: a man of some potential but little present importance. Alp now knew that literacy was rarer in the Galactic society than among the Uigurs. Illiterates did not favor literate parts, since they could not play them well, so this was an underrated attribute. Just what he needed: a potent if subtle tool for advancement.

"Here is your costume," the Machine said. Material spewed out of a slot: a loose robe falling to his calves, split at the sides and gathered by a broad belt. A short fur cape to cover his shoulders, and a fur cap. Not real fur, of course. Wide trousers, that he strapped in at the ankles. He did the same for his sleeves at the wrists. Stout leatherite shoes.

Alp knew right away that this costume was no more authentic than those of the four demons who had brought him to this time. The underwear was similar to what he had removed from the men and women on the belts, the boots were not suitable for riding, and the belt chafed. But it was a reasonable approximation, and once he wore some dirt into it he would be able to wear it comfortably.

There were also weapons, at last! A bow in its ornate sheath that hung from his belt before his left thigh. A quiver of arrows, that rested across the small of his back, with the barbs to the right. A dagger and a short sword, both in good sheaths.

He was in business. The Game Machine had admitted him on credit, which meant it thought he had a reasonable chance to repay. His choice of the part must have been the decisive factor. Apart from the literacy, he had taken Ko-lo because he had never heard of that particular chief nor his family, and he was almost certain the man had not existed historically. That meant the part was open: no specific historical fate awaited, and it was up to the player to improvise.

His memory had told him that a few such parts existed, so that the Game would not be completely fixed. There had to be leeway—room for individual initiative, along with the strict programming of established characters. No one was supposed to know whose fate was predetermined and whose was self-determined; all were mixed together in the Game. Every player could believe that he had free will.

Of course, being a free agent was no guarantee that a player would profit. Most washed out even more rapidly than the average. But a smart—and lucky—man's best opportunity was here.

This part of Ko-lo was a subchief: better than the minimum fee normally brought. That meant that immediate hazards existed that would shorten the span of play. The Machine did not say this, but in practice a peasant with a likely long life could command a higher entrance fee than a chief who was about to be executed.

But Alp did not intend to depend on either luck or the largess of an ''intrigued'' Game Machine. He happened, by the freak of timesnatch, to be thoroughly conversant with the history of the real Steppe—including particularly the ten years following the present Game-date. If the demons had thought they could profit from such information, why not Alp himself?

''Bare your arm,'' the Machine said.

Alp bared his left arm and lifted it. There was a momentary pain as light flashed. ''Your Game identity number,'' the Machine explained.

Alp looked. The light had burned a tattoo into the skin on his forearm. He was no longer anonymous!

A panel opened opposite the entrance. Alp/Ko-lo stepped out into the great Game of Steppe.

Chapter 5

SUBCHIEF

For a moment the beauty of it made him dumb. As far as he could see, the grassy plain stretched. There was not a tree or tent anywhere—nothing to interrupt the charge of a good horse. Even the door through which he had come was gone; there was nothing behind him except more plain. Glorious!

First he checked his weapons. He drew out the bow. It was not of the type he ordinarily used, being metal and plastic— plastic was a Galactic invention: a substance somewhat like dried gut, but shaped with greater versatility—rather than wood and horn. But it had good weight and spring, and the string was of sturdy nylon—yet another imitation material. The Galactics seemed to have a fetish about avoiding animal products. So it was a facsimile—but a serviceable one.

Alp whipped out an arrow from the quiver, brought it over his shoulder and nocked it in the bowstring in a single motion, as the fighting Uigur always did. And halted, amazed.

The shaft of the arrow was not solid. It was made of a beam of light. Only the head and feather were substantial—and these not very. The tip was no more than a paper shell that would collapse instantly on impact, and the nock was actually set into the feather: it should tear apart when fired. Yet the arrow as a whole had an odd firmness, and the head remained before the feather no matter how he spun it about.

How could the arrow act solid—when it was made of light? Tractor beam, his memory said, but that hardly helped.

Alp touched the shaft with one finger. Yes—that finger went numb. It was a stunner!

Carefully he returned the strange arrow to its quiver and drew the sword. It was similar: a thread of light in lieu of a cutting edge. But his experience with the police stunner—which weapon he had left in the entrance booth as a prerequisite to admittance to Steppe—convinced him that these instruments were sufficient. They would not kill—but they would incapacitate as surely as the real weapons would have.

He struck the air with his sword, shadow-cutting. He could handle it. Any player receiving a "lethal" strike would "die"—and be ejected from the Game, a loser. He could then re-enter by seeking new admittance, paying the fee, and assuming a new character. If, in the course of his prior parts, he had amassed sufficient Game-credits, he would be ahead; if not, he would have to produce the fee from his own resources. A wealthy man could afford to lose many times. But Alp himself had to prosper within this one part. His first loss would be his last, because of the waiting extradition to the hell of the chasm.

Alp found a sharp edge on the handle of his dagger and used it to mark the other weapons inconspicuously in Uigur script. A routine precaution. He brushed back his hair.

Hair? *His braid was back!*

The work of the Machine again. Players were made up for each part, so that others could not tell what they had originally looked like. Alp did not remember going through makeup, but—here was his hair, spliced as though never cut.

One more succinct reminder: he had only an idiot's notion of the capabilities of Galactic magic.

Meanwhile, the Game beckoned. The sun was high. It was noon, and the day was hot. He could relax, for all he had to do was stay alive and he would have many years' respite.

Years? Suddenly he remembered another thing about the Game: its time was not the same as that of the galaxy. The Game timescale was accelerated. Every day here was equivalent to a full year in the historical world!

So the theoretical life of a player from birth to a death of old age was in the neighborhood of seventy days. Most parts were much shorter, for they started at early maturity and often were terminated violently. Each Game hour was a historical fortnight, and each Game-minute six hours, and each Game-second six minutes.

The Game sun did not move faster. Actually, these Galactics claimed the sun did not move at all, at least not the way it obviously did. They thought the sun stood still while the plains and seas and mountains whirled around it. This was

51

yet another idiocy he would have to contemplate at leisure. For the moment he had to grasp the nature of the Day that was really a year.

This was noon midsummer—and about twelve historical hours had passed in the two Minutes Alp had taken stock. Dusk would be the fall season and night would be winter. Spring would come at dawn. He had to find a place to stay before the snows came.

That increased the other pressure on him. The dangers that had cheapened the value of the part would strike in hours or even minutes, rather than days, because of that acceleration of the time scale. And he had to make his political move within ten days—before his decade's fore-knowledge was outrun. Otherwise he would have no advantage over the other players.

He was in a much stiffer exercise of his ingenuity than he had supposed. He couldn't do much, alone on the steppe. He had to get a horse and make contact with Game-Uigurs— soon. Every day he delayed was a full year wasted!

Yet he had to waste a few minutes more. In Game-parlance, Minutes—to show their historical gravity. One day was twenty-four hours; one Day was a year. He had to formulate a strategy that would ensure his survival and bring him the greatest profit within ten days—Days. That meant achieving a position of leadership among men—and he had no immediate idea where to find them.

There was something even more urgent than leadership, however. Alp found a good sandy place and scraped a small hole in the ground. Barely half a handspan down he encountered bedrock.

Surprised, he excavated further and inspected it. The underlying material was rocklike in its hardness but was not actually rock. More metal, perhaps. Something manufactured by man or demon. So this was not real steppe.

Well, why not? This was all the stage for the Game. Underneath were those multiple layers of Galactic civilization. He must never forget that none of it was genuine, however cleverly crafted.

Meanwhile, there was his urgent business. This sand was shallow, but it would do. He squatted and attended to it, then carefully smoothed the sand over so there was no indication.

It was the longest time, historically, such an act had ever taken him.

Supposedly the Game steppe land was similar to the original geography. But not literally. The Game-steppe spanned the galaxy. This was a large canvas indeed, covering all the skies of the night, far too vast for him to comprehend fully at the moment. Smaller regions were mapped as planets—rather, planets represented cities and oases. Horses—he paused, fighting confusion as he integrated his two sets of experience— horses were space ships. Carts that spouted hot wind and flew from star to star.

So this plain was no more literal than the hours of the Day. The whole thing was a mockup, perhaps intended to give him the feel of the Game—or to lull him into a disastrous complacency. The true stage was condensed in time and magnified in scale, and the visible plain was no more than the patch of soil covered by one fresh horse-dropping.

Why should a new player be set apart like this, on foot and without provisions? Was it a handicap, a hurdle, something for him to prove himself against? If so, it was ridiculously feeble by native Uigur standards; Alp had known how to forage from the land since childhood. This land differed from his own, but he could eat grass if he had to, and if there were any wildlife at all—

No—the isolation could be a measure of protection from exploitation by established players. Every new player represented competition or opportunity for the old; suppose there were those who laid in wait to dispatch or enslave the novice? That made sense; it was good nomad logic. The neighbors must be hostile, and this accounted for the cheapness of the part.

Alp grinned in the way he had. He nocked another arrow with the skill that few Uigurs and no Chinese could match and sent it flying at a shrub on a hillock thirty meters distant. It struck a little beyond; it was sleeker and lighter than those he was familiar with, but its flight was true. He fired another, and this time scored directly.

He might be a complete novice in the Galactic city, but he was only a partial novice here in the Game—and he could fight well. He doubted that the majority of players were really adept with their weapons. Affluence and ease tended to corrupt, and these Galactics had much of each.

But the players had to interact! They had to travel from city to city—planet to planet—or remain forever encamped at one location. The true nomad did not reside alone without horse or cattle. He was part of a tribe, sharing its protection and obligation. It would be pointless to set a man down too far from such a tribe—but perhaps dangerous to place him where others would discover him too rapidly. Probably placement varied, making contact random—but still, it had to be near some locus of activity, or there would be no Game.

So he had to find that locus, before it found him. And join it on his own terms. Even if he had to dispatch a few tribesmen first, to make his point.

Where there were sedentary people or camping nomads, there was fire. Where there was fire there was smoke.

Alp looked at the sky, carefully. It was clear. No clouds, no smoke.

Of course this was the galactic year 2332 his new memory said, and the planet was governed by contemporary conventions. Pollution was a crime. So no horse dung, no wood fires. Therefore no smell or smoke. But—

There it was! A faint streak of cloud, typical of—of the condensation pattern following a spaceship moving through atmosphere! The Galactic equivalent of smoke—or the dust raised by a running horse.

The streak pointed to the south, assuming his brief survey of the sun's elevation had oriented him correctly. Therefore there was a stable there. But Alp checked the sky carefully for other signs before acting. Did many horsemen come to that oasis? Were there other places he might go, more profitably?

He found no other indications. That one, already fading in the sky, would have to do. Had he not been alert, he would have missed it—as perhaps most players did. It was distressing being afoot, and it made him feel insecure and lonely for Surefoot. But he had ground to cover in a hurry, and he would do it.

*   *   *

Alp approached the camp from the south, having skirted entirely around with inborn caution. There had been guards and at least one ambush, which confirmed his suspicion about the exploitation of new players. They had known he was coming, but they had not known his background, his life-time in the historical reality the Game only imitated. He could have killed those amateurs with ease, but he had chosen merely to avoid them.

Neither tents nor horses were anything like the real ones. He had to depend on his new memory to make the connection at all. These were one-man spaceships: long, pointed cylinders lying flat on the ground. Near them the tents were set up: nylon material stretched taut over aluminum frames, quite unlike the true nomad *gers,* but serving a similar purpose.

Alp moved in on the largest and neatest tent, certain this would belong to the chief of this party. It was dusk now, and the chill drafts of autumn were stirring; most players had sealed their tents for the winter's sleep. The camp guards were yawning: actors, not Uigurs!

Alp skulked in the shadows of the tent, alert to all camp activity as he studied the sealing mechanism. It was a strip of sticky tape that bound the flap securely unless lifted from one end.

When no one was in sight, he stepped quickly and silently forward, lifted the strip, and opened the entrance. Warm air gushed out. He slid inside and resealed the flap. He was in!

The tent was elegant inside, suggestive of the Khagan's pavilion. Certainly it was larger than any true *ger* Alp had known. Light glowed from the inner surface and from the stiff material covering the ground. There were several compartments, each sealed by one of the strips. Comfort for a large Uigur family!

Alp made his way to the center room, where a man garbed as a Game-Uigur chieftain pored over a map.

"Did you fetch him in alive?" the man asked, not looking up.

"Yes," Alp said in Galactic.

"Good enough! This has been an excellent stake-out. Does he have any talents we can use?"

"He can foresee history."

"Foresee—" The chief tapped his map, assimilating that. His body tensed, but he did not make a hostile move. He looked up. "You're not one of mine!"

"Not yet," Alp said.

"How did you get by my guards? Who are you?"

"What guards?" Alp asked innocently.

Now the chief's hand went for his sword, rapidly, as he flung himself out of his chair. He was strong and fast—but Alp's own blade gleamed first.

They faced each other, weapons lifted. The bands of light were bright in the subdued illumination here. "You can't be the recruit player!" the chief said. "Not with a move like that. You're a pro."

"I am both recruit and warrior," Alp said. "I could have killed you already—had I wished to."

The chief looked at him a moment more, then sheathed his blade. "Yes, I believe that. You must have served with the Huns and Turks in prior parts, and kept in shape. Taken a loss and had to re-enter on the minimum. Battlefield casualty? Who are you now?"

"Ko-lo the Uigur," Alp said, sheathing his own weapon but not relaxing his vigilance. He could outdraw the chief, but there could be other warriors in the tent.

"And I am Uga the Uigur, chief of this tribe, such as it is. We're currently recruiting, as you know."

Alp concealed his surprise. Uga—the man the Game Machine had questioned him about. Obviously that had not been random! Had the Machine been telling him something—or merely verifying his capacity for survival in Uga's tribe? Normally the Machine did not give assistance of any nature to individual players, unless this was required to achieve an established mark of history.

This was not the real Uga, of course. Had an armed stranger come upon *him* in his *ger,* there would have been an immediate fight to the death. The original Uga was a lusty, powerful man, who would have been extremely difficult to overcome in swordplay.

This Game-Uigur Uga was older, less proficient with hand weapons, but gifted with superior discretion. Just as well, for Alp had been quite prepared to eliminate him if necessary.

Uga spoke again. "What's this ploy about foreseeing history?"

Alp stepped up to the map. It was galactic in scale, and he could not immediately assimilate it. The lettering was in Galactic print—and he discovered to his chagrin that he was not literate in that language. For Game purposes he was no more educated than any other player, and Ko-lo's supposed literacy would be an arrow in his side.

But naturally the education helmet would not bother with the written language. This was a useless specialization in a culture where machines animated every book and kept all records. The Galactics had been freed of the drudgery of childhood study, and only dedicated scholars became scribes.

He would have to downplay that aspect of his part—and perhaps there would be advantage in concealing his Uigur-script literacy. Now he had to justify his approach to the map, for Uga was already looking at him quizzically.

"The Chinese to the south and east are less docile every year," Alp said, guessing that this was the subject of the indecipherable map. "The Kirghiz to the north are growing stronger. Meanwhile the Khagan lies about with his wives in Karabalgasun, not even bothering to inspect the frontiers."

Uga was not impressed by this political analysis. "Everybody knows that!"

So he had guessed correctly! Uga had been poring over a political chart. "In just ten years the Kirghiz will renounce their vassalage, revolt, and invade Uigur territory. The empire will fall to the barbarian. There will be no help from the Chinese, who are overtired of Uigur dominance and secretly regard themselves as our superiors. Karabalgasun will be sacked, the Khagan slain, our people driven south before the savage."

Uga considered. Prediction of the Khagan's death had perked him up. "Empires have fallen before, in Steppe. No doubt they will again. But I doubt that the rabble Kirghiz could prevail so readily over true Uigur forces, and certainly not so soon. Why, most of them are mercenaries in our cavalry."

"That's right," Alp agreed. "They have learned disciplined warfare from us—without comprehending our restraints.''

Now Uga nodded. "You put a grave face on it. But assuming this is true, and they revolt in a decade—how is it that you know this?''

"That is my secret," Alp said. "I have given you the outline; I also know the details. These are at your service.''

"Such information would be invaluable," Uga said musingly. "I could use it to achieve high office myself!" He paused. "Naturally your claim will be subject to specific proof.''

Alp showed his teeth. They had reached the bargaining stage.

"And your price will not be small," Uga added.

"A horse, a *ger*," Alp said. "Supplies. A manslave, and a woman." Alp did not feel up to remarrying so soon after his family tragedy: from respect to his lost wife he would stick to concubines for a decent interval. She, however she was, would appreciate the gesture; no new sons would pre-empt the place of the first.

"Of course," Uga agreed. "These await you now. What else?''

"Nothing else.''

Uga frowned. "I do not deal with unknown terms. What is your whole price—assuming you perform as claimed?''

"If I perform as claimed, you will be graciously inclined, and you will be in a position to exercise that inclination. If I do not, you will have me assassinated. This is the Uigur way.''

"Perhaps. Unless you perform—and assassinate *me* the moment your foresight shows the move propitious."

"I have never killed a Uigur," Alp said shortly.

"Naturally not. You have just entered the Game as a Uigur. How many Huns did you kill—as a Hun?"

Better to let the chief assume he was an experienced player. He *was*—but not in this particular Game! "I never killed my own kind. I never gave false loyalty. I never broke my oath."

"A personal foible, then. You assume I practice assassination—but you do not."

"You already have power over your tribe. You violate no oath when you eliminate the unfit. In your position, I might have to do the same."

"In real life I could not afford to believe you," Uga said. "However, in the Game reincarnation is feasible, and I have sufficient assets to select new parts with discrimination. Do you understand me?"

Alp understood well enough that this was a threat, but he had to sort through unfamiliar Galactic concepts before he grasped its nature. It took many points to enter the Game each time, and Uga had wealth in his Galactic identity. So he could re-enter immediately after being ejected . . . and seek vengeance for any betrayal. In this way the Game differed from life.

"I am not governed by fear," Alp said. "Nothing but my oath binds me."

"Every man feels fear at one time or another; it's an aspect of the instinct of survival."

"Feels fear, yes; ruled by fear, no. If I killed you this

time, I would kill you every time you returned. But it irritates me to debate nonsense.''

Uga snapped his fingers, and a girl appeared with a wineskin. She could as easily have been a warrior.

''Will you swear Uigur fealty to me?'' Uga asked, lifting the skin and squirting a purple jet into his mouth. This was a historical, not a Galactic custom; obviously he had practiced.

''Yes. So long as you live.''

Uga handed him the skin, and Alp drank expertly. The wine was strange but good.

''A pro,'' Uga murmured again, watching him. ''Just as if you'd spent your life drinking that way!'' Then, after a pause: ''And yours will not be the hand that kills me?''

''Yes.''

''You lie.''

If the man thought Alp could not draw a weapon while drinking wine, he was mistaken. But Alp did not take offence. ''Why?''

''The lives and deaths of important characters are predetermined. The Machine must enforce history in all key matters. If Ko-lo killed Uga in Asia, Ko-lo will kill Uga in the Game. You cannot swear otherwise.''

''Not unless I foresee the event,'' Alp said, impressed by the chief's cunning. ''Or unless Ko-lo is a free agent.''

Uga nodded. ''Good point. But tell me—my men were scouting the plain to bring you in, after we picked up the impulse of a new player delivery. We make use of what we can obtain, and the weak or stupid soon become slaves. Doesn't that make you angry?''

''It might make a weak or a stupid man angry.''

Uga laughed heartily "You must have real nomad blood in you! You have true Uigur pride, yet you can not be casually baited. And I guess you realize that the Machine is aware of our recruitment in this region and downgrades local entry fees accordingly. By taking you on voluntarily, I must grant you subchief status, for that is the rank your dress denotes." He gestured benignly. "Go familiarize yourself with your equipment. Here is the tent number. I will have an assignment for you later this winter."

Chapter 6

CARTOONS

It was a good horse. The fuel tanks were full so that it would not need feeding until he rode it, and the reins were not reins but still simple enough so that he knew he could manage them. The little machine that was the steed's brain would take care of the complex processes of takeoff and navigation; he had merely to direct it. But he left it nameless, unable to bring himself to call it "Surefoot."

The *ger* was well appointed, though only half the size of Uga's. It had two compartments: one for him, the other for the servants. This was not quite the way it had been done historically, but he could adapt readily enough. It would take him more time to become accustomed to sleeping on a soft pallet with sheets, like some decadent prince . . .

His manslave and woman were kneeling on the floor, awaiting his notice. He checked the man first and found him not a man but a eunuch whose tongue had been cut. Excellent! That meant there would be no offense from that quarter. He wondered briefly how the Machine found people to play such parts, as a eunuch could not be restored after the Game. But immediately his new memory corrected him: modern science/magic *could* restore a eunuch, or convert a man to a woman and back. And straight menials were not parts, but jobs. Successful completion of such an assignment qualified a person for the minimum fee next time. It was one way impoverished yet ambitious people could enter the Game, and great numbers were eager to participate on this basis. So the mutilations were temporary, almost cosmetic; they could be repaired as readily as his hair had been. And there was the chance of a great future.

The girl was young, fairly pretty, full-breasted, and did not appear to be unduly intelligent. Uga certainly provided well!

Alp intended to verify the capabilities of both servants in due course. But at the moment he was hungry. His new memory told him these servants would provide food on request, but he was conditioned never to trust the preparations of strangers when he could avoid it. There should be a store of staples in the cold-box—

There was. But it was not his type of food. Most of it was so finely processed as to have little remaining character, and the rest was alien to his Uigur tastes.

But in hunger, one could not be unduly choosy. Alp lifted out several pseudosteaks and thawed the rigid masses by dunking them in water so that they expanded into something like horsemeat. He then took them out and flopped them several times in sand, shook them off, roasted them against the incandescent filament of the tent heater, and knocked them hard against his knee several times. Only then did they approximate his accustomed fare. But this was a good deal better than nothing!

Now if he could manage to sour some milk and form it into a tasty black curd . . .

But first he had to orient himself properly, so that he could give good service when the chief tested him. That meant reviewing the Game version of history. There would be differences . . .

Every ten days—Days, or years historically—the Game Machine presented a generalized summary of events. This was done by film and TV: the window with a living picture in it. Moving images of things that weren't really there. All the summaries to the Game to date were on file in the projector's data bank—its stomach—and could be played back for reconsideration and insight. The quest for comprehension of the trends of the Game was endless among players! It would be nine days before the next summary in 840, but since what he wanted was the early part he didn't have to wait. He had only to press this button . . .

The picture came on. It was not a true window, but a flat surface with an image inside, like the reflection on a polished blade. It was in full color and seemed real, except that it was mock: a cartoon.

It showed a large man, a steppe warrior but not a Uigur, riding a horse. A true cartoon horse, not a spaceship. The caricature man carried a bow and knife and sword, but none seemed to be of fine quality. He was—Alp studied the trappings with the knowledgeable eyes of a fighting nomad and

67

historian—he was a Cimmerian, one of the ancient tribesmen of the western plains, redoubtable warriors but lacking the refinement of equipment and technique that the later Turks were to develop.

"This is Cimmerian," the image voice said unnecessarily. "He is a giant of Indo-European stock. Every so often he becomes restless or hungry, and then he rides down to the coast to annoy the dwarves there."

The picture showed Cimmerian galloping down to the coast of a great sea far to the south and east, in territory only vaguely familiar to Alp. The many little dwarves there took immediate alarm. Some stepped aside, and some tried to fight back, but none had much success against the terrible giant.

Alp stroked his thinly bearded chin. Was *this* the Game Machine's vaunted history? This ludicrous cartoon, like something a shaman might sketch on the ground? Or was some Galactic trying to make a fool of the recruit?

Alp snapped his fingers twice, as Uga had done. The woman appeared, responsive to his signal. "Have you watched this program before?" he asked her.

She looked about, confused. She thought he wanted her for that one purpose most men wanted beautiful and stupid women.

"This," he said, indicating the screen.

"Master, I have," she answered uncertainly.

Cimmerian was now beating up a dwarf named Greek. Greek was partly civilized but retained some fighting spirit. Still, he was no match for the steppe giant.

"Is this the usual presentation? Comic figures?"

She remained perplexed. "Yes, Master."

"And from this players are expected to judge the course of the Game?"

"Surely you know this is true, Master!"

Alp watched the screen again. Greek had given up the unequal struggle and taken to his ships, splitting into several tinier dwarves in the process. Each subdwarf tried to find a new home, but the more civilized dwarves resident around the little sea were not eager hosts. There was a wave of bitter fighting. One subdwarf took over the island marked Crete which, a verbal footnote explained, had recently suffered a terrible calamity that stunned its own civilized dwarf and rendered him helpless by also sinking his ship. In a few days that subdwarf took the name of Philistine and raided the fertile riverland of Egypt, but he was driven off by the resident dwarf. Then he managed to land on the coast marked Syria, where he shoved aside the dwarflings Canaan and Israel.

"This is no history of Steppe!" Alp complained. "Who cares about the bickering of the runts of the distant coast?"

The woman shook her head, unable to clarify the matter. Alp realized he should have questioned the eunuch instead; a man, even a partial man, should comprehend the concerns of men.

"Your former master—he watched this?"

"All of them watched," she said.

"All the programs?"

"All my masters."

"What happened to them?"

"They were turned off after—"

"I meant the masters, not the programs!"

69

"Some were in other parts," she said.

Other parts. So women also went from part to part through the Game and remembered past experience. No doubt this generous-bodied, scant-minded female, because of her inherent limitations, failed to rise above the minimum level. "Your last master. The Uigur." For she must have had a master in this part; menials were not set up to serve each other.

"He annoyed Chief Uga."

So Uga did eliminate opposition! Obviously he had the qualities necessary to maintain his office. It was treason for a member of a tribe to plot against the chief, but proper for the chief to keep strict discipline. Alp would not have cared to serve a weak man.

Alp had been trying to determine the extent the cartoon summaries had assisted individual players to achieve perspective. Not much, he judged. And no wonder, if they bore no closer relation to true Steppe history than this! About all he had accomplished was to verify that this *was* the official presentation . . . and that Uga tolerated no impertinence from tribesmen.

"All right," he said.

She began to remove her clothing.

"No," he said, annoyed again by her density. She would have been ideal—if he had not needed to learn anything. "That—later. Now—I want to watch the program."

She waited.

He realized that even dismissal had to be specific. "Go take a nap."

She departed submissively.

It was amazing how circumstance changed taste! Had he

known before he fell into the gorge that he would have access to such a woman, he would have assumed she was the reward of heaven. Now what he really wanted was a *smart* woman, even if she were shaped like a dead pine tree. He returned to the cartoon.

One Greek subdwarf, or possibly a related dwarf from an adjacent territory—it was hard to tell them apart, and hardly seemed important—was named Phrygia. He travelled by land, only crossing the strait from Greek ground to the land of Anatolia. That was the territory of the civilized giant Hittite, a formidable ancient warrior.

But Hittite had grown flabby in his centuries of dominance and had also suffered at the hands of the Steppe giant Cimmerian. For almost a thousand Days Hittite had reigned virtually unchallenged; now he was old and ill, and so the thrust of the aggressive dwarf Phrygia was enough to break him up entirely. The consequence of this breakup, said the cartoon voice, was severe.

Alp leaned forward, becoming interested. He had read of Hittite in the translated manuscripts and knew that that giant had been important to the later events of the Steppe. Maybe this cartoon was relevant after all!

There was now a closeup of Hittite. "Hittite was an iron worker," the narrative voice explained. "He knew how to make swords and spears of iron when others did not, and he kept his process secret. That was the reason for his great strength in battle. But when he was beaten, all the dwarves and giants began to learn how to use iron, and that changed things in both Steppe and the bordering civilized world. An iron weapon is superior to a bronze one, because it is so much harder and sharper. Even a dwarf with iron technology is strong enough to humble a giant with bronze—in many cases.

"When the knowledge of ironworking spread over the known world, the whole community of giants and dwarves was shaken up. Some giants were reduced to dwarves, and some dwarves grew into giants, and they all quarreled and fought endlessly. This, then, was the root significance of Cimmerian's push against Greek: the spread of iron technology and the consequent reordering of ancient powers."

Alp turned it off. He had not lost interest; in fact he had found the cartoon most illuminating after all, and he needed time to think about it before assimilating more. Of course iron was important; all the warriors of Steppe used iron weapons, and the skilled technicians and smiths of the mountain regions were virtually immune from attack, no matter which nation controlled the empire. Alp had not realized that old Cimmerian had been responsible, however deviously, for the world's acquisition of this blessing.

The cartoons looked foolish but were not. The magic brain of the Game Machine was behind them, its potency manifesting like the bright sun veiled by clouds. The pictures gave only cursory details on the political situation but did bring out the important fundamental points. The problem was to relate that information to current events in the Game, so as to know better than rival players how to improve one's own position.

Alp had prevailed over the four Kirghiz in part because of his superior horse and bow: that was a similar principle. In the Game there were many other improvements in weaponry;

if he failed to appreciate their nature, he would lose. So already he had profited from the cartoon insight!

Better to absorb Game history in easy stages, so that he would not become confused and misread it. He could not afford to make any serious mistake! He had ten Days to make good; while that was not much time, he could spare a couple to assimilate the past properly. His own prior knowledge of history would simplify the task.

Alp snapped his fingers twice. The girl reappeared, rubbing her eyes sleepily. "Now," he said, indicating her clothing.

She was voluptuous and tractable, so it went well enough. Then: "Hey!" she cried, confused.

Alp paused. "What is the matter, girl?"

"What are you trying to do?"

"If it isn't yet obvious, girl, it soon will be. Silence, now."

She obeyed, but it was apparent that she was unfamiliar with his technique. She was vaguely resistive despite his skill. Another Galactic anomaly: their women were unversed in the refinements of pleasure!

First the loss of literacy, now this. How much else had mankind forgotten in the past fifteen centuries?

After the girl left, bemused but educated, Alp checked the weapons he had set aside. This was a conditioned reflex with him. They were in order, except for one item: his marked sword had been exchanged for another. Uga's doing, obviously; probably the eunuch had been instructed to do it at the first opportunity. But why?

He tested the new sword and found it identical to the

original. It was not a defective weapon in any way that he could tell.

Interesting. He marked it with another Uigur-script identification so that he could differentiate it from the first. He would keep this little riddle in mind—and watch his weapons more carefully hereafter.

At night—ten o'clock in the new hour scale, the month of December in the Christian calendar—Uga summoned Alp to a private conference. That meant another person-to-person meeting, not a picture-screen interview. That also made it easier for Alp to relate, for he did not fully trust these magical communicators.

Uga was alone. "Are the facilities satisfactory?" he inquired.

Obviously he knew. Why had he taken Alp's sword? "Yes."

"Are you aware that I am not in special favor with the Khagan?"

"What intelligent Uigur *is*?"

"A clever rejoinder," Uga said dryly. "But simple answers suffice. Because I am out of favor, I am assigned few worthy players from above. I must raid recruits instead. That is a disadvantage, for there can be resentment."

Alp nodded.

"The Khagan himself is not in special favor with the T'ang emperor of China, despite all the Chinese protestations to the contrary. It is in my mind that there may be significant changes soon, and I should prefer to place myself advantageously, if you understand."

Alp merely nodded again.

"Does your ability to foresee history cover this aspect?"

"In part," Alp said. "When the Khagan dies your position in the Uigur hierarchy will be enhanced. But the Uigur empire will then be no more than a kingdom."

"All very well," Uga said. "But that will be a decade in the proving. I require more immediate information."

"I shall answer all questions as directly as I can."

"I don't want shamans' riddles!"

"Who does?" Alp answered, and that was so like the way of the shaman that they both had to laugh.

"Let's try just a Day or two ahead. I have a number of nobles in my service. Can you predict how each will act?"

This was difficult, for Alp had had little direct association with Uga's group in life and did not know all his nobles. Also, the news desired was eight to ten years old: a stiff test of memory, when so much had happened since. Finally, he had no assurance that the actions of minor characters in the Game would be identical to those of history; the Game was only a Machine-governed reconstruction, subject to many minor distortions.

"I am not sure. Some I should know."

"Intriguing limits to your powers," Uga remarked, not intrigued.

"I am better on general events. There are so many people."

"Consider Qutli."

Alp shook his head. This was just like the Game Machine's interrogation! "I know no noble of that name."

"Bilgo."

"Him I recognize. He was executed in—why, *you* killed him!"

"By no means," Uga said. "He is alive and well, a most important member of my retinue."

"Not for long! He plots against you, unsuccessfully. Perhaps you have not yet discovered this—but you will."

"You charge him with treason?"

Alp considered how to put it. "You asked me what I knew about certain men. The first you named is a blank, but if this Bilgo is the same one I remember—"

"Try Pei-li."

Alp pondered. "Him too I recognize. A formidable and loyal warrior and scholar. He will give you excellent service for many years."

"Now me."

"You?" Alp was surprised. "I do know your future, to a certain extent. But how could you believe—?"

"Where do you see me next year?"

Alp thought, putting together the events of the past, when he was a growing lad. Where had the real Uga been? "You will travel to China in 842 and not return for a year. The Khagan sends you on a mission to call on the T'ang emperor, who does not receive you kindly. There is some fighting, and after that you hate the Chinese implacably."

"I do not hate the Chinese," Uga objected.

"You will, two Days from now. I think the Khagan conspired with the Emperor to betray you, making it seem an accident. But I am not sure. Politics are devious."

Uga sat silent for several minutes—a very long time, in terms of the Game. His eyes focused absently on Alp's sheathed sword. That sword . . .

"I have told you the truth as I know it," Alp said at last,

fearing that he had in some way offended the man. "The truth is seldom kind."

"Kinder than lies," Uga said. "Now I shall tell you some truth. There is no Qutli; I made up that name to trap you. Had you given a fortune for him I would have deemed you a charlatan. Bilgo is indeed plotting treason; I learned of it recently but have allowed him to continue until I am able to determine all his accomplices. I shall surely execute him soon—and I have told no one of my intent. Not even Bilgo knows that I know—and if you were with him, you would not have exposed him as you have. Pei-li I trust implicitly; he and I were boys together in life, and he has saved my life in past parts in the Game. He keeps my records, as he is literate. As for my journey to China—I have no orders yet. We shall wait upon it. And you are either a very shrewd guesser, or—"

"It's memory, not guessing," Alp said. "But memory is still imperfect, and I can make mistakes."

"Yes. So when the Khagan sends me to China, you will accompany me."

A sensible precaution! "As you wish. But you should know: even if my memory is accurate, my information may not conform precisely to the actions of the Game."

"Because your smuggled history text may differ from the program of the Game," Uga said. "That I well understand. My interest is merely in verifying that you are in fact a scholar of Steppe history, and not a spy from the Khagan's court."

Apt suspicion, and plausible enough so that Uga would not

need to search further for the truth. "I could be both," Alp pointed out.

"Or neither. But there will come opportunities to separate your motives and your knowledge from those of the Khagan— whom, naturally, I serve loyally until his demise ten Days hence. Meanwhile we shall take you on faith. Limited faith, but it can grow."

"Fair enough," Alp agreed.

Dismissed, he left Uga's *ger*. Alp had now been in the Game several Hours, and nature had further call upon him. He walked out onto the sand, seeking a suitable spot—but a guard challenged him.

Among true Uigurs there never would have been any confusion. But Alp realized suddenly that these imitation nomads would not understand. They were not accustomed to using the sand, his new memory said. They had facilities within their tents.

All right. He turned back.

He found the place in his tent. It was a kind of chair with a hole in the top. He had heard of this type of thing; the Chinese and others used similar devices on occasion. There would be a bucket that had to be emptied periodically . . .

He looked. There was no bucket. Instead there was the shimmer of running water.

Running water! Alp recoiled in shock. It was forbidden to urinate into running water! No man fouled the precious fluid that all men had to drink!

Yet it was so: these Galactics were less than men, and this was the proof. They never buried their dung decently in sand but made a point of dropping it obscenely into this channel of running water. It was then carried down into a grinding unit that prepared the substance for "recycling" . . .

Alp left his tent hurriedly, circumvented the guard, and upheld the standard of personal hygiene he had been raised with. There were, after all, limits.

Chapter 7

MISSION

At two a.m.—February, 842—the Khagan's directive came. Within minutes Uga's small party of warriors took off for the arduous journey to China. Women, servants and tents were left behind; this was business. The blast of the jets melted long furrows in the winter snow as the horses galloped into the sky. The tiny camp was lost to sight at once, and in a moment the entire planet disappeared. These were light-speed steeds!

Uga went, and Alp, and Pei-li, and a picked body of fifteen hard riders. Uga's mission was to negotiate with the Emperor for the hand of a T'ang princess in marriage—to the Khagan. It was dubious business, as the Chinese were extremely jealous of their princesses, especially where nomads were concerned . . . More especially when Uigur power was fading. In fact, historically the mission had been unsuccessful—as Alp had informed Uga.

81

"*Noyan* to my ship," Uga said on the screen as the fleet achieved speed. Alp wondered why the chief continued to insist on this personal contact despite inconvenience, when the screens were quite adequate for communication. It was the usual nomad way, true—but this astonishing flight through reaches Alp had not before imagined had demonstrated clearly that the usual nomad ways were no longer applicable. This was not the natural Steppe; it was the Game.

But a Uigur did not answer in such a situation, he obeyed. Alp was a *noyan,* a member of the Steppe aristocracy, both in life and here.

He set the reins for rendezvous and gave his horse its mechanical head. The machine-creature made the maneuver and docked, sealing one of its airlocks to one of Uga's steed. Each horse had three such locks, so it was possible for up to four to unite in a cluster during flight. Or more, if it wasn't necessary for each to face into a common chamber. In this way no one horse was overburdened, though overall maneuverability suffered.

Pei-li docked next. The two visitors stuck their heads through the locks into Uga's ship, turning off their screens. Their dialogue was thus assured of privacy.

Pei-li's head suggested a large brutish body, that one should not draw sword against unless one intended to slay. His mouth was taciturn, his eyes watchful.

"Ko-lo is dubious about this mission," Uga said to Pei-li. "What is your sentiment?"

"A fool's errand," Pei-li growled. "We shall die in China."

"Is that your view?" Uga asked Alp.

"I do not know more than I have told you about this

matter," Alp said. "You will return alive, unsuccessful, and the Khagan will blame you for failure. Many of your men will die, and you may have to recruit from dissident Chinese horsemen on your return trip. The rest—we shall discover."

"How can you know this?" Pei-li demanded, obviously jealous of the seeming confidence Uga placed in Alp. "Do you seek to exterminate me before the fact?"

"You will also survive," Alp said, keeping his face straight.

"This is Ko-lo's talent," Uga explained. "To foresee history." He rotated his head to face Alp again. "Why should I recruit Chinese, when you say I will hate them?"

Alp had to think about that. "Perhaps it is the T'ang empire you will hate, not the Chinese themselves. Perhaps you will only *claim* to hate them. I do not know your mind, only your actions—and those only vaguely."

"The Khagan knows no more than that," Uga said meaningfully. Then he got down to business: "In the T'ang dominions—distrust the screen. Always respond affirmatively."

Alp was puzzled again. "What if you ask for information? Something that can't be answered yes or no?"

Uga smiled, and so did Pei-li, feeling superior. "Then answer as pleases you," Uga said, "so long as you stay wide of the truth."

Then Alp understood how the communications screens differed from direct speech. Others could eavesdrop on screen dialogue, so it was not to be trusted in any critical situation. This information, too, was available in his new memory; it had merely been hidden behind the more technical complexities of Galactic intercourse. So much of this demon universe was like that—concealed not so much by any veil of secrecy, but by unclear implications of its superior technology. All Galactic swords were many-edged.

The ships disengaged and resumed formation. Alp found it challenging to correlate the vast steppe and desert he had ridden in life, to the vaster volume of space he now traversed. Very soon they left the entire system that included the planet Earth behind, accelerating to a velocity his mind was not equipped to conceive. They galloped between the myriad candles of the galaxy. Their course was set for the populous center; Uga's post had been near the fringe. The entire steppe Alp had known was a mere patch on that fringe-world. It was an exercise in perspective!

China in the world was southeast of the Uigur dominions. China in the galaxy was toward the interior of the bulging disk. In each case there were mountains, rivers, bandits, deserts and other natural hazards. A desert, in Game terms, was a region of space almost devoid of planet-bearing stars, so that there was no place to stop for rest and resupply except scattered oases. Mountains were ridges of stars whose interacting gravitational wells interfered with the course of the fleet. At sublight velocity that hardly mattered—but these horses traveled a hundred light years for every kilometer a real horse might, and faster in proportion. Alp had no real concept of the length of a light year, except that it was an extremely far piece. A hundred light years amounted to about a thousandth of the distance across the galaxy. Of course the distance to China was only a fraction of the galactic diameter, but again it illustrated the proportions.

Cruising speed of the ships was actually about ten thousand light years per hour—and what horse could run a hundred kilometers in an hour? But at that velocity the space horses quickly became winded, and it was necessary to change to new steeds every hour—or to allow the old ones to walk for a period. That high speed could not be maintained in the mountain region, regardless, for a cluster of stars, each one or two light years apart, was a serious navigational hazard. The stars themselves were nothing; it was almost impossible to hit one at that speed no matter how hard one tried—and if a ship *did,* it would pass right through it at speed, unharmed. But their gravitational fields extended over significant volumes of space.

Alp shook his head. It all made sense to born Galactics, but to him it was foreign. Easier to view the dust-nebula as rivers, even if they didn't have normal currents.

At ten thousand light years per hour, the journey to the Chinese court would require two Hours, or one month historically—just as it always had. Time enough to take some rest from the sleep-helmet, except that Alp had a recent but strong aversion to such devices. So he set out to absorb some more comic-history background.

Cimmerian had a son named Scythian, and Scyth was now growing into aggressive gianthood. He was younger and stronger than his father and had little proper respect for parentage. Some dwarves openly doubted the filial relation, for parentage was always dubious among giants. At any rate, Scyth began to move into Cimmerian's territory and to shove him around. This naturally made the old giant furious—but it was far too late to undertake the disciplinary measures he should have invoked when Scyth was but a lad. So Cim had to give way.

In fact, it may have been this developing quarrel among the giants of Steppe that drove Cim down into the fringe of the territories of Greek and Hittite, with the consequent significance for the world.

Cim, however, was no giant to take that sort of bruising from an upstart youth for long. By and by he stood up and fought Scyth directly, son or no son. The two charged each other on their great horses, fired volleys of arrows, and finally dismounted to hack it with their swords.

The battle was earth-shattering (did that account for the gorge? Alp wondered facetiously), but slowly Scyth prevailed. Finally he opened his huge mouth and took a bite of Cim. Cim howled angrily, but bit by bit and bite by bite Scyth ate him, and at last swallowed him whole.

This, the cartoon narration assured the viewer, was the way giants were. Since any living thing that wasn't consumed remained a functioning entity on its own, there was no sense leaving any part of a vanquished enemy unconsumed.

For a Year or more—three or four centuries, historically— Scyth dominated the western steppe, making just about as much trouble for the civilized dwarves of the south as his progenitor had. Some wondered whether the original giant had really changed in nature at all, or merely altered his name. There was no way to be sure, since when one giant consumed another he tended to assume the attributes of the repast.

Then a third giant grew up, who may have been Scyth's own offspring—again allowing for the giants' notorious eclecticism about species perpetuation. They all, literally, were bastards. This newcomer's name was Sarmation: a bearded horseman in conventional tunic and wide trousers, with a good bow and strong arrows. He treated Scyth much as Scyth had treated Cim, and he dominated the region thereafter.

But meanwhile in the central steppe other giants were arising. This was the point where the pre-history of the Game closed, and the formal action commenced. For it was the central steppe that was the main stage.

Alp turned it off again. He could only absorb so much at one sitting. So all this had been no more than the introduction to the Game!

He checked the controls and looked at the picture of all the stars zooming by. There were more of them, now that the fleet was closer to the center; they were like bright dust motes in sunlight, beyond counting. But the ride itself was becoming tedious.

Then Uga's signal came, and they decelerated swiftly and oriented on a star, then on a planet, and finally on the Game-field of that planet. They landed, dismounted, stretched, ate, used the sanitary facilities (Alp abstained) and took fresh horses. This was a Game-depot, a Uigur post deep within Chinese territory, tolerated by the T'ang because of their alliance. In a few days that situation would change, Alp knew; meanwhile the stop certainly was convenient! His horse was worn out and could not have maintained the swift pace much longer without faltering.

This time each warrior took along a remount: a horse that would follow, riderless, until the rider needed it. For there was no Uigur post in central T'ang, and Chinese steeds, untrained to nomad rigors, would be useless.

In another Hour their journey would be over. Alp had to

review as much of the remaining Game history as he could in that time, in order to comprehend the ramifications of the current mission. Perhaps he could skip over portions not immediately relevant to his needs. He turned on the new horse's screen and settled into it, while the stars swept by outside.

The giant now being introduced was familiar: Hsiung-nu, better known as Hun. Alp considered Hun to be the grandfather of all true fighting nomads, and the example that all had followed since. He watched this sequence with special interest, his sympathies with his illustrious ancestor.

Hun lived in the middle of Steppe, and he grew up about the time Scyth did. But the full Steppe was so broad that the two hardly knew each other. There were several dwarves and a formidable mountain range between them; not all of Steppe was flat, by any means!

Hun was formed from the integration of many minor dwarves of the region. It was not until Sarmation's time that Hun really got hold of himself and ranged the area as the first full-fledged, confident giant. But then he was a real terror, because he possessed the three fundamental sources of nomad power: the composite bow, the ability to work iron, and the stirrup. The first gave him superior shooting ability, the second improved his other weapons, and the third enabled him to ride his horse at full gallop without using his hands—so that they were free to wield bow and sword on the run.

What a warrior! Alp thought in admiration. There was little a modern Uigur could have taught old Hun!

Hun's totem was the wolf, and like the wolf he was a raider. The sheepfold he eyed was the civilized bastion of

China. It was his perennial ambition to break into that rich fold, slaughter the superfluous farmers, snatch up his bounty, and escape. At other times Hun ranged the plains with his own cattle. His ancestors had once domesticated the reindeer, but climate and terrain had converted him to the horse, and only his fine animal art now reflected his former life in the northern forests. North of Steppe at this time was nothing but an icy waste; the land of promise was always south.

Hun was short, for a giant, with a stocky body and a very large round head. His face was broad, his cheekbones prominent, his nostrils wide, his ears long. The cartoon exaggerated these traits, showing how they differed from the Galactic norm. Hun shaved his head except for a tuft on top, and he wore rings in his beard. His eyebrows were thick, his eyes almond shaped, and he had fiery pupils. Completely handsome, Alp agreed.

Alp could have dwelt indefinitely on this superlative figure of a man, but the narration moved on. So Alp identified with Hun and followed the ancient nomad's glorious adventures as if they were his own—as they were, in spirit. It was his recent experience in the galaxy that was alien!

Hun, master of his own region but by no means lord of all Steppe, decided to expand his territory. He would have liked to move south, into the large fertile region below the Yellow River (Alp laughed as he saw the cartoon river: it really was yellow!)—but the giant Ch'in had just formed here, consuming the other Chinese entities much as Sarm had consumed Scyth in the west. Ch'in was now monstrous. Soft, flabby and sedentary—but so huge that no ordinary giant could budge him. Ch'in had already butted Hun's foot from inside the great northern loop of the river—an act of outrage for which any smaller giant would have paid dearly. But for the time being Hun had to expand at the expense of his weaker nomad neighbors: Yueh-chih to the west and Tung-nu to the east.

Then fat Ch'in lost his head. This was another frequent malady of giants; sometimes it led to disaster, but more often a replacement was available. When the new head was donned, the Chinese giant became known as Han. While he was changing heads, he naturally couldn't see very well, so Hun stepped across the river. But Han soon focused and pushed him right out again. The corpulent southerner was really pretty strong when he got mad, Alp ruefully admitted.

So a Month later Hun charged into Yueh-chih's territory. He beat up Yueh and cut off his head, rendering him temporarily out of sorts. Then he shoved the body westward and took over the land, only keeping Yueh's head to use for a drinking cup.

Now Yueh-chih had to go somewhere, because his horse and his cow were getting hungry, and even less important properties such as his wife were in dubious condition. So he continued west. It normally took a while to break in a new head, and Yueh's didn't think too well the first few days.

Yueh was one of a family of small giants who had moved east in the old days. Cimmerian had been his uncle, and Scythian his cousin, and Sarmation may have been his nephew. Their family was Indo-European, probably. Some of the dwarves at the fringe of Steppe called him Tokhari—but not to his face.

Alp smiled grimly, remembering. No—no dwarf dared

insult a giant directly! He probably ought to skip ahead, as Yueh-chih did not directly concern him—but he watched a while longer.

Because his head wasn't perfect yet, Yueh had trouble keeping himself together. One of his hands fell off and formed into a dwarf called Little Yueh. That one scurried south and settled in with the giant of the snowy mountains, Tibet. But most of Yueh went west across the desert. He was still a giant, albeit a lesser one, and he needed elbow room.

The trouble was, the territory west of Yueh's original haunts was occupied by another small giant. He was Wu-sun, also known as Alan. Alp remembered Alan: that giant had been the near neighbor of Tolach, father to Uigur. Alp was already thinking in terms of giants rather than tribes, even when it came to his own studies pre-dating his arrival in the galaxy! There had been several scuffles between Tolach and Alan, so Alp wasted no love on the latter. But that was a minor matter. In the cartoon history, Yueh beat Alan at first, but then Alan got his dander up and threw him out. Alan was blue-eyed and had a big red beard, and he was a fierce one!

Yueh couldn't go back east to match Hun again, so he exited west. He shoved aside another moderate giant, Saka, and continued on toward one of the territories of the powerful dwarf Greek. Actually Yueh pushed Saka right into that region, then followed him, using him as a kind of fighting shield, and Greek just had to get out. Yueh and Saka stayed there, battling the civilized giant of Parthia in the west and India in the south, and never did leave those regions.

All this had been started by Hun when he decided he needed more space. But it was only the beginning, for Hun was just achieving his first full flower of giantism. He still had a grudge against the supergiant of the southwest: fat Ch'in, now known as Han.

Every few Days Hun would get on his horse and raid Han's territory, snatching up his booty and zipping back across the Yellow River where Han couldn't catch him. More fun! Only Han didn't see the joke and even built a great wall to stop the raids. That was only partially effective.

Then Han had a bright idea. He was too clumsy to catch Hun by himself, but he thought he might get Yueh-chih to help him. After all, Yueh should have a score of his own to settle with Hun! So he sent a message-bug across the desert to Yueh. But Hun snatched the bug and held it for ten Days, just watching it squirm. At last it escaped and got to Yueh. Yueh said he liked it where he was and wouldn't go back. So the bug began the long trip home to its master—and Hun caught it again and held it for another Day. When it finally got home, twelve whole Days had passed—and it had no good news to report! Hun could hardly contain his laughter.

Those were the Days, Alp agreed, amused.

Han, furious, sent another bug to Alan, but Alan was afraid of Hun and refused to mess with him. So Han had to do it by himself. He exercised, converting some of his fat to muscle. He practiced his horsemanship and his fighting, and he actually got to be pretty good at it.

Now he was ready. Han crossed the Yellow River into the old Yueh-chih territory and began slashing around with his sword. Hun, who hadn't taken the threat seriously, had a couple of toes cut off. They turned into dwarves named

Huen-shih and Hie-Ch'u, and agreed to serve Han instead of Hun. Alp was furious at this treachery; never trust a dwarf!

A couple of Days later Han stepped right into the center of Hun's territory and really cut him up. They fought in a storm that blew sand in Hun's face; otherwise, Alp knew, the fat slob never could have done it. Pieces of Hun were strewn all about, and he was left a much smaller and weaker giant than he had been. Han set forts all through the old Yueh territory so that Hun couldn't come back, and Alp raged again at the indignity. One day Han would get what was coming to him!

But Han took no note of Alp's ire. A couple of Weeks later the dwarf living in Fergana, where Yueh had just moved out, said something nasty to Han, thinking he was beyond the grasp of the giant. Han had been dickering with him for a better horse, because the dwarf was an excellent horse-breeder. But after that insult, Han reached all the way across Steppe and bopped him head over heels and took the horse. Han was not half as flabby as he looked!

But Hun was still around, biding his time, waiting for Han to go soft again. For a Month or two he harassed Han routinely, trying to gain control of the Silk Road that stretched from Han's territory to Parthian's territory. There was brisk trade along that route. So Hun raided, taking the nice things for himself. Fine silks, precious artifacts, good slaves—rich harvest indeed!

Naturally Han was upset at this pilfering. He laid about him and chopped up several dwarves of the region who had sided with Hun, thus securing the road again.

Hun should have put up more of a fight, but he had another problem. He was not well at the moment. A routine change of heads had gone wrong, and now two heads were growing simultaneously. Each head wanted to get rid of the other and run the body. Two heads were not better than one for a giant!

One head asked Han for help. Alp took an immediate dislike to that one. It was treason to deal with the grasping entity of the south!

Han was ready enough to negotiate, however. "Certainly I'll help you," he said greasily, "if you'll promise to behave yourself. Agree that I'm the real boss of the Steppe, and promise never to make any more raids . . ."

"Go kiss my horse!" Alp muttered. But the traitorous Hun head was already slavishly agreeing. "Yes, yes!" it said eagerly. "Anything you say!"

So Han helped this head, and it succeeded in dominating the Hun body. Naturally the other head didn't appreciate this; giants were bad sports even at the best of times. "Don't give up!" Alp urged it. "You are the true head! Fight!"

But the true head's valiant effort succeeded only in breaking away a large portion of the body, which formed into a smaller giant. This lesser Hun retreated in a foul mood, beat up Alan and several dwarves, and established himself in a fine big territory north of Sogdiana. He was now called Western Hun.

A few days later Han reached out and cut off Western Hun's head with one stroke of his sword. "Vile Chinese oppressor!" Alp shouted. "He wasn't bothering you!" But the damage was done. The Hun body shuffled off and hid, not to be heard from again for over a Year.

"Now," the cartoon narrator explained, "commences the

Christianized dating system. Thirty-five Days after the decapitation of Western Hun a religious figure was born in the far west, in the same general region where Philistine had settled a thousand Days before. This event was not particularly important to Steppe, but the dating system deriving from it has been a convenient reference point for other Games, such as the recent Rome, so will also be employed here.''

It seemed to Alp that the Uigur twelve-day cycle was superior: year of the Lion, year of the Ox, Dragon, Dog . . . but the matter was unimportant.

About this time—Day 10 in the new scheme—Eastern Hun got back some of the Silk Road, because Han was having some two-headed trouble of his own. But then Hun himself had another attack of this malady. "Not again!" Alp wailed. He was somewhat disenchanted with Hun, who was showing up as less formidable than anticipated, but still favored him over the Chinese giants. If Alp had been in charge, he would have found some way to humble Han permanently!

Part of Eastern Hun broke off and became Southern Hun, while the rest became Northern Hun. It was Day 48. Both were smaller than the original Hun. Han persuaded a couple of small giants or large dwarves to raid Northern Hun. These traitors were named Wu-huan and Hsien-pi.

"Hsien-pi!" Alp exclaimed, recognizing the name. No dwarf, that!

Northern Hun, weakened by the successive breakoffs of Western and Southern Huns and now attacked from behind by his own kind, was chopped down into dwarf size himself, and no longer represented any threat to Han. The unscrupulous tyrant of the south had successfully divided and conquered the mighty horde of Steppe. Alp shook his head, disgusted.

Now a number of dwarves sprang up along the Silk Road. These were mostly splinters of the Indo-European family, related to Cimmerian and his offspring. Hun belonged to another great family called Turk, the terror of the western steppe. The little traitor Hsien-pi was from a third family, Mongol, more primitive and less important than Turk. Another family, Tungus, had little present power. All these families spoke different languages, but they could work together when they had to, and sometimes even fraternized.

A Month or more passed with constant bickering and minor scraps between Han and one of the Hun brothers, but Han generally had the best of it. In Day 93 he sent the Mongol Hsien-pi to cut Northern Hun down to size again, and around Day 155 the Mongol actually ate the Turk.

"You couldn't have done it when Hun was in his prime!" Alp muttered wrathfully. Uigur was of the Turk family, with Hunnic blood in his ancestry . . .

Chapter 8

PARTS AND PLAYERS

But there was not time enough to view the rest of the Game history; the huge center cluster of the galaxy was upon the fleet, and Hun's descendant Uigur had to deal directly with Han's descendant T'ang. The horses had to slow way down to maneuver deviously along established channels between the myriads of stars and clusters and nebulae. These were the lowlands, with a hundred Chinese planets for every Uigur planet and population to match.

They landed at the Emperor's city-planet of Changan. Its Game-surface was a fertile riverside marsh given over to extensive rice and millet culture. Stolid, bent-over peasants worked the fields, and their junks floated in the wide river. There was hardly decent footing for a horse.

Alp felt stifled here in this unnatural congestion. But he knew that his nomad impulse to burn all the buildings and plow the fields into fallow pasture was mistaken. There was, unfortunately, much to be said in favor of civilization.

The architecture was awesome to a born Uigur. Inside the palace were elegant hangings and extremely realistic murals. Uga was less impressed than Alp, perhaps because outside the Game Uga was accustomed to the opulence of twenty-fourth century existence.

The Emperor was too busy at the moment to see them.

Every Minute of the Game was six hours historically. Four Minutes was a full twenty-four hour day. Half an Hour was about a week. The Uigur envoys had traversed a major section of the galaxy to call on this derivative of fat Han—who was now entertaining himself by making the nomads wait. Alp showed no more emotion than the others did, but he seethed.

A full Hour passed, and another commenced.

The Uigurs were vastly outnumbered here, and by protocol had no weapons inside the palace. They had to wait the Emperor's pleasure.

After a full historical month, Uga talked as privately as was possible with his lieutenants. "It's a studied insult," he said. "How should we best react?"

"We must wait," Pei-li counseled. "We dare not return without an answer for the Khagan."

"The only answer the Khagan wants is news of Uga's death," Alp said. "We know he will get no T'ang bride. Why should we tolerate this lowlander insolence? There is nothing to be lost by a little judicious violence."

Pei-li, no coward, shook his head negatively. "On honest open plains I would fire an arrow up the Emperor's fat posterior. Here in his home-city it would be disastrous to try it. Our corpses would not even be honoured."

Spoken like a genuine Uigur! Alp thought, liking the gruff noble better. Of course the matter of proper burial was academic; there were no literal corpses in the Game.

Still, his own time was running out. Alp had to achieve a good position within ten Days or lose his advantage and probably his life. He could not afford to sit idle far from the sources of Steppe power while that precious time expired. "Neither of you will die on this tour," he reminded them. "With no legitimate mission to accomplish and no risk—"

"I do not care to gamble the fortune of my part on the word of a recruit player," Pei-li said shortly.

Uga spoke quickly, preventing Alp's response. "Ko-lo's counsel is tempting—but if we survived we should not know whether it was the result of Game predetermination or sheer luck. If we die, no one would care. So we shall let discretion guide us and wait."

So they waited. After the third Hour they went out to look at the city—and discovered T'ang troops surrounding their horses and men.

Uga's jaw tightened. "Do they think mere *Chinese* could hold us if we choose to leave?" he snorted. But he made no overt issue of the matter.

More time passed. When the palace attendants became openly insolent, Uga finally had enough. "Inform the Emperor we shall see him now," he said, walking toward the throne room.

Guards appeared, swords drawn. Alp and Pei-li, unarmed, moved as one man to flank the chief on right and left and shield him with their bodies. Uga forged straight ahead, pushing through the archway leading to the throne room.

Weapons flashed. This was the pretext the palace guards had been waiting for: a technically aggressive move against the Emperor. Alp, on the right, leaped right, his boot sweeping up to catch the wrist of the attacking guard and kick free the descending sword. Pei-li, on the left, blocked the left-hand guard with a length of wood he seemed to have smuggled in, disarming the man similarly. Suddenly the two Uigurs were armed!

Uga, true to his diplomatic mission, left his own hands open. He pushed through the archway.

Now a dozen more guards converged, blades lifted. But Uga marched on as if oblivious to danger. Alp and Pei-li turned to face the men behind, but had to keep pace with their chief by marching backward.

Two T'ang guards charged. Alp, now defending leftward because of his backwards position, had to parry awkwardly from his right. His sword met that of his attacker—and blue sparks crackled where the two blades came together. Alp yanked his own back, and the band of light re-formed. This was an uncommon variety of swordplay, and he didn't like it! Was it impossible to parry a stroke?

But Pei-li was showing how it was done. When a Chinese sword came at him, he rotated his own so that the flat of it made contact—and the other sword bounced off, its light-edge momentarily disrupted. Then Pei-li struck—and though the light sliced through the guard without visible effect, the man toppled, stunned.

Three more guards charged. This became ticklish, because

while two were being fended off, the third could strike Uga down from behind. Alp turned his sword sidewise and put all his force into a sweep that knocked his man's weapon into that of the center man, fouling the thrust of each in a shower of sparks. Pei-li, meanwhile overcoming his own man, then sliced across both guards engaging Alp and dropped them to the floor.

Pei-li might be gruff of speech and sharp of suspicion, but he could indeed fight—and that was the important thing. The man's technique was distinct from Alp's, but by no means inferior. Not all Galactics were decadent!

Still Uga marched on, paying no attention.

With five of their number out of the Game, the remaining guards were more respectful of nomad prowess. They followed closely but for the moment did not attack. Alp appreciated the guards' tactical problem: on a one-to-one basis the Uigurs were supreme; but when the Chinese ganged up they crowded each other and became vulnerable in another way. Yet they had to protect the Emperor—or suffer consequences perhaps less pleasant than elimination by sword.

They were still in an anteroom of this capacious palace. Uga parted the heavy curtains shrouding the entrance to the throne room proper and stepped boldly through as Alp and Pei-li waged another defensive action against the furious lunge of four more guards.

The vast room was empty. The throne was bare.

"Not even here!" Uga said, disgusted. "Probably carousing with young boys in some other decadent city. Bastard never intended to see us!"

"Might as well go home," Alp said, glad the scheme had been exposed, so that no more time would be wasted.

"Not without a damned princess!" Uga said.

Pei-li shook his shaggy head. "I agree with Ko-lo. The Emperor will not give us a princess—especially not after this mischief in his palace. We have dispatched eight—"

"Nine," Alp said, running another through.

"Who said anything about *giving?*" Uga demanded, cheerfully grim. "Are we not Uigurs? The Chinese exist only to provide spoils for the sons of the Turk!"

Alp was getting to like this man, too! He might be imitation-Uigur, but he had the basic spirit. Uga's eyes-front march to the throne room had been an impressive act of nomad bravado. The Chinese would remember that!

But Pei-li counseled caution again, even as his sword dazzled another guard. "Reinforcements will come soon. We are surely finished in these roles if we delay further before going for our horses."

"Ko-lo says these roles of ours cannot be terminated here," Uga said. "Do you now call him liar?"

Alp knew Pei-li had been observing his technique, just as Alp himself had been observing Pei-li's. Pei-li was more proficient with this particular type of weapon at this time— but Alp's strength and reflexes were faster. Was Uga trying to set them off against each other?

Pei-li stifled an explosive bark of laughter. "Not while I yet live!"

Alp relaxed. Pei-li had identified the essential conflict: they would have to die to prove Alp wrong. It wasn't worth it!

"*You* two won't die here," Alp said, parrying another aggressive guard. "Unless the Game diverges from history. But *I* have no such assurance. My own future is blank to me."

"Still," Uga said, as if that were a mere quibble, "we might as well put it to the test." And he walked forth into the bristling blades of the Emperor's reinforced guard.

Pei-li and Alp, caught by surprise, were not able to protect him immediately. The T'ang troops were astonished. They fell back, daunted by the assurance of the unarmed nomad who stepped so blithely into their midst.

Now Alp was quite curious. The theory was simple enough: the Game Machine would not permit an important character to die unhistorically. But the practice could become complex. What would happen if a guard struck directly at Uga, and no one was there to foil it? Alp had observed no direct intervention, and all characters in this play seemed to possess free will. So how *did* the Machine preserve the lives of those players fated to live—and how did it ensure their demise when the proper time came?

Uga strode on through the ranks, Pei-li and Alp following. The guards, abashed, did not attack. There was now an aura of invincibility about the Uigur group. Did the guards suspect that the Game plan protected at least two members of the party? Were the Chinese afraid of what might happen if they pushed that limit too hard?

The question bothered Alp increasingly as he followed the chief. History was too intricate; there *had* to be control if the Game were not very quickly to diverge far from history. Yet there was *not* control—and little diversion so far. Some element was missing.

He could test it very simply: all he had to do was try to slay Uga himself. The Machine would either act—or it wouldn't. But he *couldn't*—because he had sworn loyalty. Aside from the fact that treachery against one's leader was not the Uigur way.

But he was a special case; most players were Galactics and so not bound by true Uigur codes. They would try to get ahead by cheating.

Then he saw a possible solution. In life, death was final. In the Game, it was not. A player could assume a new part—and no doubt an old part could be reactivated by a new player. If Uga died here, a new Galactic would be sent in to fill his place, and Game-history would continue with only a momentary hiatus. Who else would know the difference? The *part* would terminate when history decreed; the *player* remained mortal. Despite his overall immortality!

They had been taking ridiculous chances! How many other players had thought they were untouchable—only to wash out early, while replacement players reaped the fruits of their labors? The Game Machine didn't care about people; its concern was the proper re-enactment of history.

Uga walked rapidly from room to room of the great palace searching for his princess, while the guards followed help-lessly. Less helpless than they knew, perhaps! But this brought up another problem. What would happen if they actually found the princess? Success of this mission was not fated, either!

Obviously they would not find her. The Emperor would

not have left a royal daughter here while he departed. So this was futile, if Uga would only recognize that.

Uga shoved aside the curtain of an upstairs chamber. A girl screamed. Alp felt a shock of alarm before reminding himself that there would be a thousand servants and slaves here for every royal figure.

She was a child about nine years old—but a black-haired regal beauty. "Who are you?" Uga demanded, striding into the room.

Though terrified, she put up some show of hauteur. "I am the Princess Kokachin, and if you don't get out of here—"

"Take her," Uga said to Alp.

". . . my father the Emperor will have you—"

Alp moved to sheathe his sword—but had no sheath. For the moment this minor problem upset him more than the major one: they *couldn't* take this princess!

". . . boiled in oil," she finished defiantly.

Uga took the blade from his hand. "I've passed up some of the fun; now it's my turn to fight!" he said. "And if what you predict is true, I couldn't get her out of here anyway—but maybe you can!"

For Alp had a nonhistorical part . . . maybe it would work, after all! Uga wasn't going to take the girl to the Khagan; he just wanted to punish the Emperor. Would the Machine allow that variation?

Chapter 9

KOKA

Meanwhile, the immediate problem. Alp knew the little princess would not come willingly. She had meant her threat literally. But at least this represented a fair test of Game policy and might offer insights that would assist his private effort. He grasped the girl by the arm and leg and heaved her over his shoulder.

He expected her to kick and claw and bite, but she didn't. Apparently it was beneath the dignity of a princess to fight, even a child-princess. Dire threats would have to do! Or perhaps she was now terrified into immobility—though she didn't *seem* afraid. But she really had little to fear; the palace guard would surely rescue her long before the Uigurs reached their horses.

Now it was Uga and Pei-li who wielded the swords on either side of Alp. If they wanted to ditch him, now was their chance. He was almost helpless, for even the nonresisting burden of the young girl was too heavy a load to permit effective combat—even if he had his sword. And it was death to any common man to touch a Chinese princess; that was a policy of centuries.

But the guards, strangely, remained cowed. They followed closely but did not attack again. Why weren't they fighting and dying for the princess?

"I think you're right," Uga said to Alp as they moved out of the palace. "The mission is phony. We can't be killed— but we also can't steal a princess."

Alp looked at him, perplexed. "We seem to be doing it!"

"She's a double, obviously. Worthless."

Then Alp's captive began to struggle. He needed no further proof of the accuracy of Uga's suspicion; the decoy could expect no mercy from the raiders when exposed! But Alp hung on to her, determined not to risk the counter-ruse: princess impersonating a decoy, and thus getting away.

"I have resources to re-enter the Game even if I take a loss in this role, as you know," Uga said. "It was worth the risk to see whether your foreknowledge was accurate. I believe it is; we should otherwise all have been killed in that fracas. The princess-ruse is the Machine's way of keeping the script straight; we can't be killed here."

Alp decided not to voice his new suspicions about the risk to players as opposed to roles. It was only a notion, and perhaps an erroneous one. They *had* survived an impossible situation; that could not be coincidence!

"But even with foreknowledge, you can't avoid your fated termination," Pei-li said. "What can this gain you?"

"What can it gain any man to play the Game?" Uga asked in return, rhetorically. Galactics played it because of the thrill of adventure without actual danger, the experience of living in times not their own and dying without death. Every person who wanted to take the stage could do so, this way, living his part. "Little is truly fixed in an individual player's role, for only the high points of his historical prototype are known. I must live and die in the framework set for me—but I can achieve a greater or lesser status, depending on how well I manage my affairs. And I can manage better if I know the limits set."

Which was about as clear a resolution of the conflict between individual initiative and the mandate of history as Alp could have asked for. He still wasn't clear on the method of scoring the Game, except that the better a player's position at the time of his elimination, the higher his score. Alp had to earn enough to both pay off his debt to the Machine and buy a new part so that he could stay in the Game indefinitely.

They reached their ships and pushed through the guards ringing them. Still no one tried to attack. Because the Emperor wanted the Uigurs to think they were getting away with the abduction? This bad acting could hardly fool smart nomads! Or was it because the Emperor wanted a good solid pretext to sever his alliance with the Khagan? No—this had been arranged with the Khagan; the pretext was merely to eliminate Uga. Perhaps it had proved to be too expensive in manpower to do the job in the palace, so they were holding back while they set up a more economical system.

It was a play within a play, really! All they could do now was see it through. Uga mounted his horse, and Pei-li and

Alp went to theirs. Uga checked with his riders by screen and gave the order to take off.

And the Chinese let them go.

The spare horses, on slave-circuit to the ones being used, failed to rise. Nothing could be done while in flight; their remounts were lost.

Alp didn't like it. The T'ang troops were not *that* cowardly nor the Emperor that stupid. It would have been far easier to wipe out the small Uigur party outside the palace by filling them with arrows from ambush. It wouldn't matter if the pretend-princess died too; they could have spread the word about the attempted abduction and how it was aborted. This had the aspect of a more devious trap.

"Let's get home in a hurry!" Uga said to all his men on the screen. "Our remounts slipped the leash, so we'll have to economize. Fastest route is through the fringe of that dust-nebula we passed on the way in." For a moment Alp's map-screen lighted, the nebula centered. It was, of course, impossible to look directly at an object that far away; all they would see would be its appearance of several years ago, because of the time light took to carry the image. "It's worth the small risk of collision with particles," Uga continued. "Follow me!"

Had the man lost all nomad caution? The T'ang troops could intercept a direct route anywhere, at their own convenience, and massacre the party with minimum commotion.

No—that had not happened historically, for the parts of Uga and Pei-li continued for several more years. Neither the original nor the Game Uga were fools. The Uigur party had to escape.

Maybe the T'ang Emperor had set some sort of trap calculated to catch the nomads in the seeming abduction of a royal daughter, resulting in a seemingly brilliant tactical victory over the fierce Uigur warriors. That would be good for many Game-points, surely! While Uga hoped to outsmart the Chinese by seeming to fall into that trap—and then escaping dramatically. Points there, too. Now it all made sense.

In this technologically magic universe, words could be overheard from far away—particularly those transmitted by screen. Therefore the really important words were never spoken on the screen; real business was done in person. Alp had gone along with the Game conventions, but only now was the larger rationale behind those conventions coming clear.

The Chinese ambush should be just beyond that dusty nebula, not far outside the congested galaxy center. It was growing larger in the screen-replica. The T'ang horses would be hidden by it even if there were no delay in viewing it, for the dust was thicker than it looked. Right now those troops would be moving into place under that cover, guided by Uga's careless mention of the nomad's route home. All very neat and clean—and if anything went wrong the Emperor would express complete ignorance of the matter, saving his face.

As the complex politics of this simple trip developed, Alp discovered that he rather liked them. This was the kind of machination he understood, and he was ready to challenge the ingenuity of fat T'ang just as he would have liked to do with fat Han or fat Ch'in. All Chinese giants were very much alike, and all were legitimate prey for nomads.

Now he considered the princess. She was jammed into his horse, slowing it though her mass was not great. He would be at a disadvantage in combat, and his horse would give out prematurely—and she wasn't even genuine! What should he do with her?

Now that he had time to study her, he observed that Kokachin was a very pretty girl despite her youth. Her nose was tiny, her eyes bright, and she had delicate features. She was not afraid of him and he liked that.

"You're awful strong," she said. "Gee, this is exciting!"

Childish prattle! But he liked her looks and her spirit, for she could have passed for a true Steppe girl. Most Galactics were too large and flabby even to be mistaken for Uigurs, in spite of the skillful makeup of the Machine; she fit the part well.

"I suppose you know there will be danger," he said. "We'll have to evade or fight off a T'ang ambush, and many men will die."

"Sure," she agreed. "If it's a significant engagement, it'll be worth several points to me, and maybe I'll be able to afford a better part next time. Someday I'd like to be a real princess!"

The ambush loomed, for they were accelerating toward it as if unaware. But she had touched on a matter Alp's new memory did not cover clearly: the system of point-scoring in the Game. "How would that work?" he asked.

"You know. The influence weight factor. If I affect you, and you're important in history, I get a percentage of your total even if I'm not important myself. Maybe I can fall in love with you and save you from execution or something and you'll be the next barbarian Khagan and be worth a hundred thousand points and so I'll get maybe ten thousand and be able to buy into a real empress part next time!''

So that was the way it worked! Points for influence! ''I don't think I'm going to be a Khagan, but you can still fall in love with me,'' Alp said.

''Gee—*can* I?''

''If that's what you really want.'' It might be cruel to play her along, but he wanted to be sure she didn't get balky about giving out this vital information. She did not desire success half as much as he did! ''How many points would you get if I were only a chief?''

''Well, that depends,'' she said seriously, not seeming to find it strange that he had to ask. That was the beauty of childish naiveté! ''If you were chief for a long time, and you married me as first wife, I'd get quite a few points because I'd be pretty important to you.'' She paused. ''Or do you already have several wives?''

This child had forthright ambitions! ''Only one—and she was killed.'' Fifteen centuries ago—and still it hurt. How much better it would have been had he lived long enough to exterminate more Kirghiz!

''Oh, I'm glad!'' Koka exclaimed. ''Oops! I mean that's too bad . . . uh . . .''

''Let's figure it out together,'' Alp said gruffly. ''How many points do you think I could be worth, and how many would that make you worth, and how good a part could that buy you?''

''That's easy! You get one point for every Day you survive in your part in the Game, just as I do. So let's assume we both last twenty years—that's a base of twenty points. That's reasonable, isn't it?''

"Certainly!" he agreed, and she smiled. Yes, there was nomad blood there.

"Then you get a bonus point for every ten men you have under you each year. How many do you have?''

Oh-oh. "I used to have three hundred—but then I suffered reverses," Alp said. He didn't explain that the reverses had been the overrunning of the Uigur empire by the Kirghiz, back in real history before he had come to the Game. "Now I serve Uga and don't really command men myself. That might improve; depends on the next few battles.''

"Oh," she said. "Well, let's say you win, and get back all your men—that's thirty points a year. And then if you live twenty years, that's six hundred. Plus your own personal points, and any you get for influencing history. It might amount to a thousand points, and if I were your first wife— you wouldn't raise any other wives above me, would you?''

"Of course not," Alp said reassuringly.

"Then I'd get maybe two hundred, plus my own points. About two hundred and fifty all told. The entrance fee for a genuine princess is one thousand. So if I had several good parts like that, I could work my way up in a century or so.''

"Still, that's a lot of points," Alp said. "You might not marry a chief every time, you know.''

"I know. But it's fun hoping!''

"Just how successful can a single part get, if everything goes well?''

"Well, I think Attila the Hun amassed half a million points. And that wasn't even in Steppe, but way off near the

114

European fringe where they have all those squabbling princi-palities! So a *real* leader should . . ."

Attila the Hun! Alp knew that name only deviously, through his scholarly researches before the fall of the Uigurs. The man must have fared better than the homefolk knew! Yet the Game history showed how the giant Hun had been decimated and his power destroyed by fat Han and the traitor Sien-pi. Had Western Hun pulled himself together for another major effort, or did Game history diverge entirely from real history, thanks to the effort of some ambitious player? He would have to review the rest of the cartoon presentation and find out!

Meanwhile, he had gained the information he craved. He set himself a target: one thousand points to be earned in this part. Then he would be able to re-enter the Game in style and amass more next time, continuing until—

Until the Game ended and he had to return to the galaxy? To be deported into the chasm?

"First we'll have to make it through this battle," Alp said grimly.

"After we win that will you marry me?"

Alp was flattered by her single-mindedness. "You're young, yet."

"But I'll grow!" she cried. "Oh, please, I'll never get abducted again! This is my only chance to break out of the palace-menial circuit! I could be a real good wife to you, and I'd never complain no matter how much your barbarian *ger* stunk—"

"My *ger* does not stink!" Alp snapped. "And I'm no barbarian! I'm a literate Uigur chieftain."

"Gee, even the Emperor can't read!" she said, awed.

Alp saw that he had made a mistake. First, he was not literate in Galactic; second, he thought it best not to let others know about his ability to read historical Uigur. There might come a time when he had use for that talent. "All right," he said to distract her. "If we live through this battle and make it back to the Steppe, I'll have you betrothed to me, for marriage when you're of age. How does that sound?"

"Great!" she exclaimed.

Actually it was no promise at all, for many early betrothals came to nothing, and much could happen in the four or five years it would take her to mature. But she had helped him more than she knew, and he would not be averse to marrying an attractive girl like her—if that was the way it worked out.

Then he remembered that they were speaking of only four or five *days*, Game-time. History was accelerated, but surely not human beings! She would still be a child . . .

But now the most pressing problem was sheer survival. In Minutes they reached the first fringe of the dusty nebula. It was a large one, with arms of opacity extending out in several directions, separated from each other by a hundred light years or more. Here Uga's horse slowed—and as they touched the diffuse dust, Pei-li's horse broke away from the party along with five other riders. They disappeared into the dark body of the nebula.

Uga, Alp and the ten remaining troops passed straight on through, traveling in a looser pack so that the overall diameter of the nomad posse was about the same.

They continued at decreasing velocity toward the main mass of the nebula. Alp was grateful for this, for the bank of instruments beside the controls told him his horse was tiring. The extra weight of the girl Kokachin . . .

"All present?" Uga inquired on the screen.

Alp recognized his cue. "All present," he replied. His instruments had picked up Pei-li's departure—but dust and distance would have concealed it from the Chinese.

"No sign of pursuit?"

Another demand for an affirmative response. "None."

"In what condition is your horse?"

For that the applicable directive was: answer as pleased him, always staying wide of the truth. Uga had anticipated, with true Uigur cunning, just such a maneuver as this. "Plenty of pep—but I've dismantled my bow for cleaning, since we're in the clear."

Uga chuckled. "Those Chinese have neither courage nor skill enough to bother us; you won't need your bow at all! We'll raid a T'ang outpost for new horses and maybe some recruits. Where's the captive princess?"

"I transferred her to the horse of one of the other men; he's got her on cleanup duty. Don't tell the Khagan!"

Uga laughed explosively. What an insult to the eavesdropping Chinese! Even though they knew the girl was no princess, Chinese face was being lost, because officially she was Kokachin.

"I'll catch up on sleep now," Uga said. "We'll just be walking the horses for a while. Don't interrupt me for any reason."

That was to make sure Alp understood, and kept full alert—and *did* notify Uga at the first sign of trouble. "Right, Chief!"

Uga's face faded. "Why did you say I was on another ship?" Kokachin asked.

"So the Chinese won't know how tired my horse is from the extra weight," Alp explained. "That will throw off their calculations when they fire at us."

"Gee, you're smart," she said admiringly.

"Better hold the compliments until we come through this alive," Alp said. But he was flattered again. She probably understood the need for such ruses as well as he did, but wanted to make him feel superior. That was a very promising trait in a girl.

If she had wanted to mess him up, she could have screamed a warning while he had the communicator on, and the Chinese monitors would have picked it up. Apparently she really had thrown in her lot with the Uigurs, hoping for faster advancement that way. A sharp girl, ready to take advantage of any break offered in her quest for Game points. She could be a real help to a man with similar motive, especially one who lacked proper familiarity with Galactic society and conventions.

Alp knew he was rationalizing, trying to justify his promise to betroth her, since he never broke his given oath. This lacked the status of an oath, of course, but the principle was similar. Yet he would not have made that promise had he not liked the look and sound of her, young as she was. The beauty of a nomad girl was a fleeting thing, best caught early so that none of the bloom was wasted. In five years Koka would be lovely; in ten she would be fading. Then it would be time for younger, fresher wives.

Except that it would take her about three-thousand-six-hundred-and-fifty-days to age ten years—and that would bring the Game up to Day 4,500 or so. Even five Years would bring it beyond the present Galactic date! Kokachin might flower in some other Game, but hardly this one.

Alp shook his head sadly. The chances that he would live to see her beauty were not good.

Chapter 10

BATTLE

Now they were upon the nebula. Alp hoped the other Uigur riders had been briefed as he had been, for surely the T'ang trap was about to spring.

The dust of the interior was not nearly as thick as it appeared from a distance. Stars were visible within the nebula, and at close range space seemed empty. But they had to slow way down to navigate it safely, for as with a river the visibility was deceptive, and it was thick with small rocks that could interfere with the ships. The galaxy outside faded out, and they were in a small private universe.

Then, in the center, Uga abruptly diverged. Alp started to follow him, but realized after an instant of reflection that he should maintain the original course. The ambushers had to have a fleet to attack, or they would become suspicious and perhaps thwart the counterattack.

Four ships accompanied Uga, leaving six with Alp. They spread out to approximate the original fleet perimeter—but that ruse would soon become obvious when they left the shade of the nebula and engaged the enemy. If the T'ang caught on too soon . . .

Alp checked his bow. In a Game like Armada, his memory told him, the ships mounted laser cannon that fired bolts of searing light. This did not actually harm the target, but did stun the occupants, partially or fatally, depending on the marksmanship. It amounted to the same thing: elimination of the inept or unlucky. But this was the Game of Steppe, and this ship was not a boat but a horse, and Alp had to depend on his personal bow, modified for space. This meant mounting it at the firing window and changing the arrows to laserheads. A computer-magic screen helped him aim, for no human could approach the precision necessary to orient on a target light-seconds distant.

"I can read off the chart for you," Kokachin offered.

"And betray your own Emperor?" So far her cooperation had been passive; could he trust her beyond that?

"I never saw him. I just made beds for his concubines."

"Even concubines have beds?" Alp asked, amazed.

"Sure! And most of them never even get used."

"The beds? Then where—"

"The concubines, silly! Big waste, if you ask me."

This was drifting from the subject. "All right, you can read the chart—if you can read."

"Numbers I can read, and that's all you need, isn't it?"

His memory agreed. Galactics were number-literate, after all, perhaps because combinations of numbers were essential for directing the many machines. "But if you call off wrong corrections, they'll shoot us down instead of us getting them, and your part as well as mine will terminate at a loss."

"I know," she said, for the first time showing nervousness.

The reduced fleet emerged—and an arrow passed within range of the ship's perceptive field. They were already under fire.

Alp watched the screen. Two bright lines appeared on it as the computer tracked the paths of the multiple-lightspeed arrows. The enemy could not know the nomad's precise location yet; they must have been firing randomly at the estimated zone. That suggested that they were well equipped, for these were sophisticated and costly arrows. The stun-beams were only triggered when the solid units were proximate to the target, as a lightspeed beam could not hope to catch a ship traveling at hundreds or thousands of light years per hour!

Alp did not return fire. The ambushing ships had a fair notion of the location and velocity of the nomad fleet because they had been indirectly tracking it all along, and it was Alp's job to be where the nomads were supposed to be. But the Uigurs could not pinpoint the enemy horses until more arrows had been fired. By the time the T'ang ships showed up on the vision screens, they would be far beyond the visible points. It was a tricky business, estimating where a given ship would be and doing it accurately enough to score!

A third streak registered—and this one projected back to intersect one of the prior streaks. Now Alp had a recent fix on one enemy ship! But still he did not fire, for the moment he did so the enemy ships would correct their markings on

123

him and zero in properly. Tracing arrows was the surest way to nail a horse and rider.

Alp spurred his mount and the ship accelerated rapidly despite its extra burden. This would make it look helpless and scared, when its jump forward was calculated by the enemy. The six Uigur steeds behind him followed, spreading out further and losing what little formation remained. A mathematical formation would be disaster; the moment the enemy nailed one ship, they would have the others pinned by magic projection.

The T'ang troops would be closing in now, sure of their prey. The range was too great for either side to operate effectively. Proper combat range was light seconds, not light minutes. And the coup had to be complete within the two-Minute period of Game daylight, when all instruments were functioning efficiently, or the prey would escape in the night.

It bothered Alp that the ratios were not consistent; a horse could travel at many times the speed of a historical horse, and much farther before resting; yet the time-scale for days and seasons was maintained. But the Game Machine had compromised wherever it had to, limited by human adaptability more than anything else. Alp, like the other players, usually ignored the four-minute cycles of the days, except in specific cases like this where they became critical.

More blips showed as the misses became nearer. Some were ghosts: unverified locations that the computer projected on the basis of the probable T'ang formation. The Chinese military command never had mastered the strategy of disorder; that was why it was normally so inept in battle against true nomad cavalry.

The jaws of the T'ang trap were closing neatly. But where were the teeth of the Uigur countertrap? These had to bite too, or Alp and his few riders would be finished. As the enemy drew closer, their aim would improve, until finally they would come within a fraction of a light second and in straight visual range. Evasive maneuvers could prolong the battle, but only rank incompetence on the part of the Chinese would allow the Uigurs to escape cleanly. Alp's only protection was the T'ang's ignorance of the true disposition of the main nomad fleet. For of course the Chinese *were* incompetent.

Alp glanced at Kokachin. Her little face was drawn. Obviously she had never been under fire before, and of course she had the tremendous liability of being female. Adventure in space was fine to dream about, but the reality could be terrifying. Even Alp himself was nervous; he had fought many times in circumstances only superficially dissimilar, springing bandit traps and such, but always felt the tension of incipient injury or death. His old wounds pained him sympathetically.

He would not be able to spot the horses of Uga and Pei-li when they attacked, because they would be too far away and their arrows would not be directed at him. But he would know by the enemy reaction to the counterambush!

"What if they desert us?" Koka demanded shrilly. "They could just sneak home while we get wiped out!"

"That is not the Uigur way," Alp said. But he too felt unease. These were not true Uigurs; they were merely Galactics playing a Game. How could he be sure of their motives? "Anyway, the T'ang would know that not all of our ships were accounted for, so the ruse wouldn't work."

"The others would still get a good head start," she said, wanting to be convinced it was not so.

She was right, and it was small encouragement. Alp chided himself for being entirely too trusting. He had let himself become lead decoy on his first mission for Uga, and he was certainly vulnerable. If Uga broke faith, Alp would be finished—and he had no assets to re-enter the Game and seek revenge.

"Uigurs do not deceive their own," Alp said.

"They're better than Chinese, then!"

The enemy bolts abruptly stopped. The screen showed that no further arrows were entering detection range, and the probability of that happening accidentally in such a battle was small. It meant Uga had attacked from the outside! The T'ang fleet, surprised in the rear, was reorienting to protect its flank.

Alp cut his drive. Now he could rotate his ship, bringing his bow to bear more accurately on the enemy positions while resting his horse—who sorely needed it! He could not afford to drift long, as the enemy could readily orient on him after he fired. But he wanted no distractions the first time he used his bow in space.

He focused on the lead T'ang ship on one side. The second ship in his formation would orient on the second, and so on as far as they lasted. Meanwhile the formations of Uga and Pei-li would be firing too—and with luck the Chinese fleet would be wiped out. Trap and counter-trap: normal international relations!

Alp fired and knew that this released the other players in his group to do the same. The twang of his string was a mere formality; it was the aim of his arrow that counted. The head of it passed through the window and jetted away under its own power, accelerating phenomenally. Each arrowhead was a miniature spaceship, unburdened by the weight of a man and his attendant equipment: food, air, communications, safety features, weapons and so on. It could move at a hundred thousand light years per hour, catching any ordinary ship—provided it was properly aimed. A shot that missed did not cross the galaxy in an hour; it soon fizzled out and became a dead meteorite, its propulsive and stunner power expended in the futile quest for the target. No doubt the omniscient Game Machine had means to recover and recharge the lost hardware.

The target screen showed the calculated course of Alp's arrow. That line crossed the indicated T'ang blip, showing Alp's aim had been good—but there was no way to tell whether contact had been made. A direct score would make the enemy ship go dead, and in due course the Game Machine would salvage that too and return the stunned occupant to the mundane galaxy. If the ship did not return fire, Alp would assume he had knocked it out.

On the other hand, if his shot had missed—as it probably had, for the enemy would be foolish indeed to remain in the same course after firing—there would shortly be more accurate return fire.

Alp cut in his drive and bucked his horse into a random evasive pattern. This was an uncomfortable type of warfare, when he saw his enemy only through an electronic magic pattern on a screen and had to wait for the other rider's shot before firing his own! How was the superior warrior to prevail, except by blind chance?

"I can't correct your aim," Koka said. "It was right on."

FLASH! An enemy arrow passed within half a light second, illuminating his board. Alp felt the momentary vertigo that signified a fringe-range swipe by a stunner. The T'ang bowman was right on the job with a lucky shot.

Alp watched the line-projection on his screen. It did not appear instantly complete, though the arrow would have passed faster than human perception could trace it. The limiting factor was the small computer's computation of its course. Thus the line extended back to its source and crossed another line three light minutes away. That ship was approaching rapidly, orienting exclusively on Alp now—a bad sign. Had it already dispatched the other Uigur ship, the flank attacker?

FLASH! Half a light second again—and Alp had not yet returned fire! Such accuracy was impossible, in the face of his random evasive pattern!

But now Alp had two extremely pertinent fixes on the enemy. He fired his arrow, then cut his automatic pattern and let his horse drift, watching.

"On target again!" Koka exclaimed. "You're some shot!"

FLASH! A full light second this time—but still too close for chance. In fact, had he not cut his program, that enemy arrow could have intersected him! That meant—

But it was so highly improbable that a random program would be intersected by chance that that possibility was not considered in battle tactics. Space was too large . . .

Alp yanked out the program spool. He had set it himself, as another matter of innate caution, before coming to China, though at the time he had hardly understood its function.

This was not his spool! This lacked the Uigur-script identification. Another had been substituted.

He stared at Koka. But she could not have done it; she had been with him all the time, she could not have messed with his controls without his knowing it.

Uga again? For an instant a raging suspicion took him. But it cooled as he worked it out more thoroughly.

The T'ang had sabotaged his horse. They knew his evasive pattern! Only the slowness stemming from Koka's added weight had thrown the ship off that pattern, making the shots miss. Had Uga changed that pattern, it would have remained random as far as the T'ang were concerned.

FLASH! Yet another close shot—but two light seconds distant. Because he was drifting, no longer even partially on that deathtrap spool. He had not fired since commencing his drift, so there was no indication the enemy could pick up. By that thin margin also he had averted elimination!

Now he started up again, throwing his horse into a manual evasion. What, then, of the other nomad ships? Were they all vulnerable? No—only the ones that had been left unoccupied. His, Uga's and Pei-li's. Unless the other Uigurs had been put under stasis and released without being informed—difficult, but perhaps possible with contemporary technology. No—the Game Machine would not permit such modern techniques in Steppe! Still, none of the ships could be assumed to be secure!

Useless to call Uga. Either the chief had been alert enough to catch it himself—or he was already dead. Alp became angry.

He checked the position board, orienting carefully on the

enemy ship whose location was now obvious because of the four fast shots. But he did not fire. He accelerated his own ship there instead.

"Hey, this is fun!" Koka exclaimed, terrified. "Why don't you fire back?"

"Because I'm using original Uigur strategy," Alp muttered grimly. "The T'ang never saw this before . . .."

"I have a sudden premonition of futility," she said.

Fancy language for a little girl! But Alp could not pay attention to her now. In an instant he was there.

His computer's calculator was pretty good; he passed only a fraction of a light second behind the T'ang ship and was able to pick it up on visual. It could have reached him as readily but obviously had preferred to fire at the unrandom pattern from a secure distance instead of evening the odds through close combat. Immediately Alp set his own ship on inertia, spun its nose around to aim toward the other, and shot his arrow.

It missed by a tenth of a light second. He had aimed too quickly and made a bad shot, considering his range. A stupid, amateur failing! He had to maneuver again, before the other could reorient. He accelerated—directly toward the enemy.

FLASH! A bolt passed him, missing by a scant three thousand kilometers, a hundredth of a light second. Sparks danced across his control board and his screen went momentarily blank. For an instant Alp lost consciousness. But he fought out of it; a stun ricochet had struck his spine and deadened his legs, but he could still control his horse!

Then he was there, a hundred kilometers from the other, so

close collision seemed imminent. He read the screen himself, foggily interpreting the indications, drawing back his bowstring. He fired almost without aiming, trusting to his lifetime fighting reflexes; it seemed impossible to miss at this range.

This time he saw the flash as his bolt scored. The light was for tracing only; the invisible stun-component passed right through the vessel and wiped out the horseman.

The T'ang ship was dead, its horse riderless. "What do you think of that, Koka?" Alp cried gleefully. "This is just like old times, when I came up behind the Kirghiz—"

He paused, glancing at the girl who had not answered.

Kokachin was unconscious, and he knew she was Game-dead. The beam that had struck his back must have been in line with her head.

She had had such exuberant notions, and perhaps she might have made good on them. She had already gotten him to go along with a proposition of marriage! Now she was out of the Game.

Chapter 11

TRUST

Uga and Pei-li survived the battle; they had checked their own equipment and discovered the traitor spools. Eleven of the fifteen riders came through it also. Nomad strategy and sheer fighting ability had prevailed over T'ang deception. Comparison of notes brought the conclusion that there had been thirty T'ang horsemen, thirteen of which had been dispatched. Alp himself had accounted for three: Game-vengeance for the death of a Game-friend.

"Not bad for a Uigur action," Uga muttered, "but not good. Better to have wiped out every one of them."

They were, at any rate, now in the clear. The Emperor would have no chance to set up another ambush before they won free of his territory—and the Chinese troops would not be eager to fight again after sustaining such a reverse. They had thousands more available horsemen, but such loss of face hurt them severely.

Alp was tired. He had not slept since arriving in the galaxy, and he had been hard-pressed before coming to the gorge. The partial stuns he had sustained weakened him also. But he could not relax yet.

They raided a T'ang depot for fresh horses, and Alp left the pseudo-dead pseudo-princess at the planet for recovery by the Game Machine. He hoped she had the resources to make it back into the Game, even if her new part lacked promise. He had known her hardly an hour, objectively, and of course she had been only a child, but she had also been a lively person and he had liked her. Perhaps it was the probability that he would never see her again that made the abrupt separation so poignant. Perhaps it was her evident nomad traits. But he decided it must be her naïve ambition, so like his own though less desperate. He *understood* her motivation—as she might have understood his.

Uga now divided his small fleet into three groups, each of which would post its own lookout while maintaining visual contact with its own members. That was an extremely tight formation, but since each group would be maintaining a random-variation course and staying off the communications screen it seemed safe enough. Near the Chinese capital such proximity of horses would have been suicidal, as one barrage of arrows could have knocked out all of them.

Alp assigned his lookout, gave his horse its head—i.e., locked on to the group course—and turned to internal problems. He had to sleep—but he also had to view the remaining history of Steppe. He also had to divert his mind from the unmanly sadness that congested his chest since Koka's loss. He remembered how his wife had passed; that had been a different world, but not different enough.

He turned on the cartoon history, stretched out in the ship, and set the sleep helmet over his head. Suddenly he was dreaming.

Hsien-pi was now a full-fledged giant. He took over all the territory Northern Hun had had, and fired a few arrows at Alan for good measure. Alan just stayed where he was, avoiding trouble.

Han had uplifted Hsien-pi, but the new steppe giant was of inferior character. Soon he was trading blows with his bene-factor. Han beat him back—but Han was getting old. His strength declined as his corpulence increased; he grew ill, his head fell off, and three new heads tried to grow in its place. One head won out by Day 285, and the Chinese giant was called Chin.

Alp turned his head in sleep, and the dream faded in a tumble of dwarves and beheadings and internecine conflict. After a time he turned back—and found himself in a struggle with a giant insect. No, it was only a giant, Juan-Juan, whose name in Chinese meant "unpleasantly wriggling insect," and he had taken it too literally. But there was no doubt this giant had power!

Alp was Uigur, and now he recognized the other giant as Avar—and he was a Mongol! It galled Alp to be subservient to this inferior breed, but he had no choice. Avar controlled the old Hunnic empire. So Alp's attention flitted westward, seeking Western Hun and Attila.

After Hun had lost his head around the beginning of the

Christian era he disappeared into the western reaches for a year or so, recovering his strength. An Indo-European giant named Goth came down from the far northwest and occupied territory to the west, while Alan lived south, with several dwarves around. Beyond these, farther to the west was the huge civilized giant Rome, who had taken over all the territory once occupied by Greek and Egypt and Hittite and Philistine and others.

Alp remembered the indignities he had suffered at the hands of old Han a Year before. Rome was another rich, fat, civilized nonsteppe giant encroaching on the prerogatives of the true nomads. Alp's own land was drying up and his cow was thirsty—but he couldn't move his Hun body west into the fertile lowlands because Rome selfishly barred the way. Well, this time Alp was in charge, and Hun would not suffer such indignity a second time!

He moved west and beat Alan, who broke into two parts. One Alan-dwarf agreed to serve him; the other fled westward. Then Alp-hun attacked Goth, who fell into three parts, each a small giant: Ostro in the east, Visi in the west, and Gepida. Ostro-Goth and Gepida submitted to Alp, while Visi-Goth fled west along with Alan. Alp could have caught them, but it suited his purpose to let them go.

Visi and Alan charged right into Rome's territory between 350 and 400—and lo! Rome had become too flabby and confused to stop them. After that, all the other small giants charged in, hacking chunks out of big Rome—and Rome himself fractured into two halves! In the process of fleeing from Hun, the fugitives had done Alp's work for him.

Now it was time. Alp marched into Rome's territory himself. The half named East Rome couldn't stop him and had to hand over a big chunk of land. Then Alp moved on into West Rome's section, for he knew from the Chinese experience that no part of a civilized giant could be trusted not to make mischief eventually. Alp tore things up, battering Rome heavily, until Rome landed a lucky counterblow that made him pause. Ah well, and next Day Alp raided another section.

But on the third day after that Alp's bold Attila-head fell off. He was blind—and in that moment of incapacity his subject-giants revolted and beat him up. "Oh no! Not again!" Alp cried in anguish, reliving the battering fat Han had given Hun so long ago. He retreated a couple of steps in order to grow a new head in peace—and two heads grew instead, and before he knew it he had split into two dwarves, Kutigur and Utrigur, who immediately started fighting each other. Avar, meanwhile, watched from the east, ready to move over and subdue them both once they had weakened each other sufficiently.

Alp gave up in disgust. It was impossible to change the basic nature of giants! He returned his attention to his own, Uigur.

"Throw the Mongol off!" Alp cried—and in Day 508 under his direction Uigur did just that, rebelling from Avar's dominion. But eight Days later Avar returned to cut off Uigur's head and make him vassal again. Five days later Uigur tried another revolt but didn't succeed. So in 545 he got clever and enlisted the help of his Turk cousin T'u-cheh. "Together," he whispered, "we Turks can finish the Mongol!" But T'u-cheh pusillanimously warned Avar, and Uigur was foiled again.

137

After that T'u-cheh, whose name meant "strong," conspired with another giant against Avar, and beat Avar and drove him out, and took over his territory. Alp-Uigur, who had started all this, got nothing; in fact he now had to be vassal to the other Turk!

Alp had a headache. This business of forming empires was fraught with pitfalls! But he kept trying—and after many further ups and downs Uigur succeeded in throwing off Turk dominance and prevailing over the other giants of Steppe. At last he had come into his own—in 744.

Uigur became allied with T'ang of China. Uigur provided most of the military power and T'ang most of the civilization. But soon Uigur himself became civilized, literate, and altogether too nice for his own good. He took to painting pictures and playing music and writing books. He invented his own script. He got religion. He became the most educated giant Steppe had ever had.

Alp woke refreshed. Now he understood the Game. The cartoon summary and his actual experience in life plus his knowledge of the next several years gave him a useful advantage. But all too soon the Game would catch up!

He had to have new information on the future! But how was he to obtain it?

The Game Machine knew the full course of events. It could run the summary all the way to the end. If it were possible to outwit the Machine and get a copy of the full Game plan—then he would indeed know the future!

That, actually, had been what the four original demons had been trying to do, in their way, when they fetched him here! Now he had some sympathy for their position. They had gambled ingeniously, stepping right out of the framework of the Game. Had they succeeded in fetching a man from a century in the Game-future, instead of a mere decade—and had he been more amenable to their management—they could have scored tremendously.

Demons? They had been bold men, risking everything to get ahead. His kind. He could deal with them now—and perhaps he should. They were out of the Game, having lost all their resources in the time-fetching effort, so they should be eager for a chance to earn back some points.

But players were not permitted to step blithely in and out of the Game. They entered formally by registering with the Machine and paying the entry fee, and they departed when their parts terminated. How had the four demons gotten below? Had they already washed out—or had they had active parts waiting for exploitation, the moment they returned with their information?

Regardless, Alp had to maintain his present part, until he acquired enough points to buy in again. Even if he did reasonably well this time, he had little assurance that his next part would match that performance. He needed a good long-range insight, so as to be able to select superior parts and multiply his assets.

The framework of the Game spanned the entire galaxy. So did the contemporary civilization. How were the two kept separate? On an individual planet it was simple: the Game was played on the sealed-off upper level, the Gameboard. But in space—what was to prevent a ship from crossing over, one way or the other? Could he ride his horse right into the other framework and back?

No, his memory informed him. The Game pieces were marked, both animate and inanimate, keyed to the Game universe. And the galaxy used efficient thousand-passenger ships to cross space, not one-man horses. Attempted cross-over would set off an instant alarm. Few if any sneaks succeeded.

But Alp was not an ordinary player. He had a scheming Uigur mind. Now he had a notion how to do it.

"You foresaw accurately," Uga said, back at their homecamp. "We failed—but survived—and now I do feel a certain antipathy for the decadent T'ang. I do not like traps—when they are laid against me."

"I told you nothing that was not already plain to you," Alp said.

Uga smiled. "No, you told me much. Had you been an agent of the Khagan's, you would have seen to it that I died in China. Instead you fought hard and well—very well!—on my behalf. I never saw such a demon in battle!"

"Still not proof," Alp said. "I could not void the Game plan for your part any more than the Emperor could."

"Yet you can participate with greater or lesser enthusiasm. I watched you, while I tempted you. I am satisfied. You have the true nomad spirit."

True, necessarily. But how would this Galactic know? "In your position, I would not be satisfied," Alp said.

"I have proffered you my trust. Why do you not accept it?"

Alp had already wrestled with this problem and come to his necessary conclusion. To accept trust was to return it—and that added a dimension to the problem. The Uga of

140

history he would not have trusted—but the Uga of the Game was of different stuff. "I will tell you my story. Trust me then, if you can."

And he summarized his situation as honestly as he could. Uga listened at first with obvious reservation, then with intensifying interest.

". . . and so I came here, using my knowledge of these ten years to impress you," Alp concluded. "But very soon the Game will pass my time, and my usefulness will expire. I might have conspired with that girl Kokachin to extend it, but she—"

"She only played a part," Uga reminded him.

"Yes, of course." But still that something nagged at him. Pointless infatuation with a Galactic child who was out of the Game anyway.

"I believe you," Uga said. "There are mysteries about you that only such origin explains. Such as your acceptance of my leadership despite your obviously superior qualities. You—"

"Why should I not accept it?" Alp asked, puzzled. "All my life I have served inferior men, most notably the Khagan himself. In the framework of the Game, I must obey the Game-chiefs, even as I did historically. At such time as I am a full chief, I will expect the same service to me."

"That's what I mean. You knew my men were out to ambush and enslave you, and you escaped that, yet you hold no rancor. A Galactic would not feel that way; he would scheme for revenge, as I shall scheme against the Emperor and against my own Khagan."

"You acted as any Uigur would," Alp said. "You will

conspire against the T'ang but not against your own, despite what you say in the heat of betrayal. I schemed to enter the service of a capable leader, but on my own terms. Why let new players go to waste?''

"Thus you are a true Uigur, standing out amid the false ones. I could not fully trust a Galactic, sad as that commentary may be.''

Alp agreed privately; something had been lost in the centuries, or perhaps it was merely the inevitable decadence of civilization. "There may soon be a Galactic playing the part of Alp,'' Alp said. "He will die suddenly, though he won't know it. Would you trust him?''

"Unlikely! And I think you'll be better off if you resist the morbid temptation to meet that player. You may not much mind my rendition of the historical Uga, but it could infuriate you to see yourself misplaced.''

"Yes. I shall stay away from him—and from his wife.'' Uga refrained diplomatically from commenting, and in a moment Alp changed the subject. "Now you know I am not a Galactic. Before, you did not know. Why, then, did you proffer your trust?''

"Look at your sword,'' Uga said.

Alp drew it out. This was the blade Uga had provided for him, not the one he had taken from the T'ang guard. There was still nothing unusual about it.

"You would not be equipped to appreciate this,'' Uga said. "In your world, every weapon is unique, and you know it by the feel. Here they are mass produced, each identical to the other, and not made of metal at all. You would not necessarily know which one you carried.''

"I know you changed the one the Machine issued me," Alp said. "But yours seemed as good, so I made no issue."

Uga laughed. "So it *was* Uigur writing on that handle! I am illiterate, as are most successful Galactics, but I saw those little scratches almost by accident and I wondered, Pei-li told me it was not Galactic writing. Either it was accidental, random abrasion—or you were literate in some unknown script. I remembered your finesse with that sword, and I pondered . . . but the whole thing seemed too far-fetched to entertain seriously. We have time travel, but it is prohibitively expensive unless the object fetched is returned to its origin soon—and you weren't."

"Now you know why!" Alp said. "I speak and write Uigur; I cannot read Galactic."

"That figures—now. Those helmets teach only what the common citizen needs to know. Incidentally, don't depend on that instant education too much; it fades more rapidly than real knowledge, and only lasts a week or so. You hang on to what you need by using it, like the language, but the rest passes."

"But why did you exchange my sword?"

"A routine precaution—the same kind you take when you mark your weapons. I had no special reason to trust you, especially when your fighting skill was so evident. Note the color of the light-edge as you hold up the blade."

Alp noted. "Pure white, like fresh mare's milk. Pretty—though not as pretty as a true blade."

"Now tell me a lie—and watch that light."

"I enjoyed your personal concubine thrice while you slept," Alp said.

The sword-beam flashed red as he spoke.

"You never lied to me," Uga said. "The blade was your monitor."

Alp looked at the sword, keeping his face neutral despite the fury he felt. Why hadn't he been alert for that?

"Don't feel bad," Uga said benignly. "You could hardly anticipate every wrinkle of a technology fifteen centuries after your time!"

But this was a wrinkle that had been current in the stories of magic Alp had known as a youth! He *should* have anticipated its reality in this universe of magic. "Is it infallible?" he asked. "Some men can lie with a straight face, so that no one knows what is in their minds."

"Test it and see."

"I enjoyed your concubine only once," Alp said. The light changed. "I didn't enjoy her—she is old and ugly." Still the light was red. "Like your wife." It flickered. "I enjoyed *my* concubine." This time the light went white. "She is husky and stupid." White. "A stupid woman makes the best wife." It flickered again.

"Half truth," Uga said. "Stupid women make good nomad concubines but tend to bear stupid children. Conflict of interests there."

"The child Kokachin was not stupid . . ." Alp said, and the sword was white.

"So you see, your straight face cannot fool the monitor," Uga said. "It is based on principles you would not understand. It is keyed to your brain waves, not the muscles of your face and body. If you can tell right from wrong—if you know you speak falsely, it knows. If you lie without intent to

144

harm, to spare someone's feelings—we call that 'white lying'—it shows pink. And if you intend to kill by treachery, it turns black.''

Alp put away the sword, noting how its light showed through small holes in the scabbard. Uga might not be a true Uigur, but he was admirably cunning! ''Pink for a white lie,'' Alp muttered. ''And white for a pink lie?''

''Now I have revealed the secret of my power,'' Uga said. ''How I can recruit strangers yet avoid betrayal, and how I know when the Khagan plots against me—if I have a chance to substitute the weapons of his envoys. Even the Game Machine does not know what I have done with these weapons—or if it does, it has not taken steps to prevent me. I am a laser-medic in life, and rather skilled . . . I charge you not to betray me, as I shall not betray you.''

''I shall not betray you,'' Alp said, not looking at the swordlight. ''That is inherent in the oath of fealty I made you.''

''But that was before I exchanged your weapon. I was unable then to verify—''

''I do not lie at the behest of a weapon!'' Alp said angrily. ''I lie only when dealing with enemies, as is proper.''

Uga shook his head, smiling. ''That Uigur code of honor— how I admire it! But don't depend on it among Galactics. They are not made of the same stuff as you.'' He paused reflectively. ''But all this is mere diversion. What is on your mind?''

''I must do well in the Game. Well enough to be able to enter another part when this one ends. And another after that, until—''

"Until the Game ends and you can enter another?" Uga frowned. "This is perilous. Your identity would be subject to thorough scrutiny at Game's end, and you would not be allowed to continue to the next. If you really want to survive beyond Steppe, your better bet is to purchase a Galactic pardon, so that you cannot be sent back."

"A pardon? For what?"

"For your origin. For entering our framework illegally. Since it was not entirely by your own choice, you should have some legal basis for your plea. But with enough money you can ensure success. Our governing council is forthright about such things."

"Graft?"

"Naturally not!" Uga said with another smile. "Merely a monetary facilitation. We are civilized!"

"How much?"

"Much, I'm afraid. Perhaps half a million Galactic points."

"I would have to be Attila!" Alp exclaimed, appalled.

"Perhaps you can be. With foreknowledge—of course Attila is past, but there must be other conquerors coming." He looked at Alp shrewdly. "Surely you have something in mind."

"I can not foresee events beyond my own time," Alp said. "But I think I might learn these—if I could leave the Game for a while, undetected."

"Leave the Game? Without a stake for re-entry?"

"*I* leave. The part remains. When I return, with new information—"

Uga was thoughtful. "You are an aggressive thinker—a man of my stripe, I flatter myself. You wish to maintain your part, so there is no record of your absence and the mundane police will not be alerted.''

''I also wish to play this part out to the end, for it seems to have good potential—especially if I achieve the knowledge I need.''

''How do you plan to sneak out of the Game? The Machine is a regular mother hen; it keeps close watch.''

''I think it would be better if you did not know. My attempt may fail, and if you are implicated—''

''I am already implicated! The police would have everything from your head, believe me! Even if you died before capture, they would analyze the chemistry of your brain and read off pertinent memories on a computer printout. Besides which: how can I help if I do not know?''

''I require no help. Just an understanding of my motive, and patience.''

Uga nodded. ''Spoken like a true—oh, never mind that! You have sworn service to me within the environs of the Game, and you have no proper existence outside it. So your profit is my profit, until my part terminates naturally. If you should come anywhere close to achieving an Attila, my association with you should reward me greatly. Apart from the fact that I do have a certain moral responsibility for your welfare, so long as you are my man. Suppose I send you on an isolated mission of indeterminate length, to another region of space, perhaps bearing a report to the Khagan—''

Alp shook his head negatively.

''To some foreign court, then. You could visit the fabulous Byzantine—''

Alp shook his head again.

147

"No," Uga decided. "I need you nearer to me. A mission to another section of this planet, which happens to be your own Earth, one of the springboards of humanity. Unsurprising, considering that it was a timesnatch that brought you here, not a spacesnatch! A secret mission—no company."

"I may be gone two Days—or forever," Alp warned.

"Two years—or indeterminate," Uga said, unconsciously modifying the statement. "I wonder—purely hypothetically—how a man without identity or economic resources or even any lasting knowledge of Galactic society might succeed in obtaining information made available to no other person—even those who have made it their avocation to outsmart the Game Machine? There would seem to be prohibitive obstacles."

Alp realized that he would have to trust Uga a little further. The man was not questioning his motive or his integrity, but his ability—and had accurately identified the weakest aspect of his scheme. "He might locate the demons—the men who brought him to this universe—and use their time machine to fetch a document from more recent history—before the Games were instituted. Such a document could reveal the historical future."

"Clever, very clever," Uga said appreciatively. "But not clever enough. I might tick off several excellent reasons why this would not work."

Alp stared at him gravely. "What reasons?"

"First, it might take many days or weeks to locate such people, assuming they remain on the planet. And longer to convince them. And yet longer to arrange financing for such a mission into the past. Time snatches are costly under the best conditions, and subject to many limitations both legal and paradoxical, and payment is required in advance. Even prominent archaeological ventures have difficulty raising the fees. I fear the Game would be over before the information was obtained.''

Alp had been primarily concerned with the first problem: escaping the Game secretly. He had planned to work out the other stages of his project extemporaneously. Now he saw that forthright Uigur scheming had no place in this complex galaxy.

"Still, there might be a way to avoid that hurdle,'' Uga continued after a pause. ''The four men do not really need to be located. They expended their resources—mostly on bribes for key officials, I suspect—and are out of the Game. They intended you no favor, and you owe them nothing, any more than does a white rat who escapes the scalpel. All that is really required is the time machine—and all that is ultimately required for this is sufficient Galactic assets. As it happens, I have sufficient.''

"Then you hardly need success in the Game,'' Alp pointed out.

''You don't comprehend the motivations of affluence,'' Uga said. ''I *do* need that success—as much in my way as you do in your way! The man who has wealth without success is not complete. I am a very capable technician with useful connections in the field, but not at all a hero. Only the Game offers that notoriety I crave. And you, perhaps, offer the means to it.''

So Uga wanted to be cut in—and was making a fair offer. ''You mentioned more than one objection to the plan.''

"The document would be bound by the normal limitations of paradox," Uga said. "It would have to be completely lost to history, so that its absence would make no conceivable difference, even to some later archaeologist who might excavate the grounds and discover it. In short, one that was destroyed soon after loss. Such a document would be extremely difficult to locate, without special knowledge—" he paused. "But you *have* special knowledge, don't you! And since it should be feasible to snatch the document, photograph it, and return it within seconds, there would be no potential interference historically and it could remain for the archaeologists . . ." He trailed off, musing it out. "Still, the computers are all keyed to alert the Game Machine the moment anyone attempts researches of this nature, and the Game Machine is an extremely sharp artifact. So unless you know precisely where and when to look—"

"I don't know those things," Alp admitted. "But I am certain of this: the document we need will be written in Uigur script. Uigurs are the only educated nomads extant, and there are no likely prospects to succeed our place. Other powers may come and go—but they will employ Uigur scholars, rather than training their own. And I am literate in Uigur."

"You're right!" Uga exclaimed. "The Game Machine would keep track of all translations into Galactic, and of all serious scholars of Steppe history and language. But you are not a part of our society; there is no record of your capabilities. The Machine can hardly have allowed for a literate Uigur national! No library research, no translation . . . if we could locate even one native paper, just enough to suggest the politics of the future . . ."

"What are your other objections?" Alp asked.

"I don't see how you plan to escape from the Game. Or to return to it, undetected. The Machine keeps most careful track, and all players are numbered."

"We need dead men. Two or more. The Game patrol will locate them and pick them up and identify them and pass them down into the regular world. But if a substitution is made just after identification—"

"Ah! Riding the dead! That could work—if only because nobody ever tries to sneak *out* of the Game, and so the Machine won't be alert for that. But there are still complications. What happens to those dead men when they wake and find themselves still in the Game? The paralysis lasts only a few hours. And what about the hard part: getting *back*?"

"Choose men you can trust to keep silent. Perhaps the same who will fill our Games-roles during our absence. The Machine will not check them while they live. When the time comes to re-enter, pay the fees and enter as new characters—minor parts. Your own recruiting net will bring us in. Then change places with the two listed dead—"

"And they will be as well off as they ever were, in new parts!" Uga cried. "While there is no record of our temporary absence! Beautiful! By the time the error in their identities is discovered, twenty Years may have passed, and it will be impossible to unravel. They themselves won't know the complete story. Pei-li will have to know, so he can cover for us in the Game; that's all."

Alp didn't like cutting another person in but saw no help for it. Someone *did* have to cover. "But we shall have to find a way to remove our own identity tattoos," he said. "At least temporarily. Otherwise the Machine will see—"

"Skin graft. Elementary."

Alp smiled. "You say you are no hero, yet there is surely Uigur blood in you! Now you are answering the objections!"

"I daresay there is Uigur blood in every man of the galaxy, technically! There was a great deal of interbreeding once massive interplanetary colonization began, with the multilight drive. I know I have Chinese ancestry—and there was Steppe blood in that, certainly! And after observing the similarity with which our minds work . . ."

"Perhaps we will both be Khagans," Alp said.

"But let us never war against each other!"

Alp smiled agreement. But he knew that whatever parts they took in future, the Game would be followed. There could be no lasting personal loyalties . . .

Part Two

MONGOL

Chapter 12

REVELATIONS

The document was almost illegible, hardly more than a charred fragment. The photograph reproduced every smudge, discoloration and tear with marvelous fidelity, but still the chore was difficult.

"It is Uigur script," Alp said. "But not the same as the style I know . . . more evolved, I think. And so many passages blotted out . . ."

"But you *can* read it!" Uga cried eagerly. "There must be some hint—"

Alp read, painfully: ". . . taken from the manuscript of the five Uigur envoys . . . followed camel tracks across the desert for three days . . . race of ox-footed men . . ." He looked up sharply. "I recognize this! My grandfather was in the retinue of the exploration party that went north and west to gain information about the territories surrounding the em-

155

pire. They came to a land of summer snows where men hunted on snow-shoes—but it was hard to make this plain to the folks back home who hadn't seen such footwear, so they described it as . . . what a foulup!''

"Not a foulup!'' Uga said. "Mythology in the making! This document must date from after the Uigur time, so that the author misread the comparison and took it literally. Maybe that's how all myths begin! But if this is a page of mythology—''

Then their effort had been for nothing. Rather than admit that, Alp went back to the reading. ". . . a tribe of great shaggy dogs with human wives, descended from the union of a princess with a dog come from heaven. The women gave birth to human females and canine males . . .''

"This is potent stuff!'' Uga said. "Did your grandfather explain that one?''

"He said the men were dark brown and of mongrel visage, covered with hair,'' Alp said. "The women were catlike in shape and doglike in manners. Those people hunted with dog packs and had a canine totem; they had a legend that their first dog was hatched from the egg of an aged vulture.''

"Amazing!'' Uga said. "Mythology feeding on mythology! But still, if there is no actual history—''

Alp looked ahead. "Here is the compiler: This summary of Khitan folklore was prepared the summer of the Year of the Dragon on order of Jenghiz Qan, Lord of the Sons of Light among the Mongols and Master of the World, by Tata-tunga the Uigur.''

"When would that be?'' Uga asked. "What year?''

"The cycle of animals goes twelve years,'' Alp said.

"Surely the Khagan can't be a Mongol!" He had a long-standing contempt for all the tribes of the Mongols.

"We must go where history leads," Uga said more philo-sophically. "Who are the Khitans? They must have power too, if their folklore is being recorded."

"The Khitans? A minor tribe of the Mongol family."

"I think we have the information we need!" Uga said. "The Khitans can't be minor for much longer! This Jenghiz Qan who rules them—even if the title is exaggerated, it points the direction of history. We have to get Khitan parts, and watch for the birth of a baby named Jenghiz—and keep an eye out for the Uigur scholar Tata-tunga too, for he will lead us to Jenghiz! You and I and Pei-li—three chances to land what may be a really major part!"

Alp nodded regretfully. "We must seek the Mongol."

In 840 the savage Turk Kirghiz threw off Uigur's control and invaded his territory. Uigur was chopped into dwarf-size, and he fled south, his glory gone. In 847 he lost his new head in battle, again.

"Where is the Khagan?" the others asked as Alp and his battered party returned.

"Khagan Uga is dead," Alp said grimly. "We must re-treat again." In the future the literate, educated dwarf Uigur would have to be content to serve other giants by handling their written work. His days of empire were done.

But the new Khagan, distrusting Alp's philosophy and his affiliation to Uga, had him assassinated shortly thereafter. Alp did not even know what killed him. One moment he was leading a patrol near the shrinking border; the next there was a fierce pain in his back . . . and then he was reviving in a Galactic chamber, feeling the prickle of stun-recovery all over.

"Your Dramatic Balance for the role stands at 610 Points," the voice of the Machine said. "From this is subtracted 100 Points advance against prior admission fee. Positive balance of 510 Points."

Alp was quick to reorient. It had only been seventeen days, objectively, since he left the entry booth. Even in Game terms, he had not survived very far beyond his own historical time. But because his help had enabled Uga to become Khagan after the Kirghiz invasion, Alp had made a decent score. "That means I can take another part!" he exclaimed.

"You have five days grace period in which to make selection without leaving the Game. Entry fee is payable before selection and is not refundable."

Alp understood that much. After five days he would be booted out into the galaxy—where the police waited. Certainly he wasn't going to change his mind after paying the new fee! But it would be smart to use those free days to rest and reorient, so as to enter the new part in a suitable frame of mind. Seventeen days—yet it seemed like so much longer!

"Your Audience Quotient for the prior part is now available," the Machine announced.

"Let's have it, then," Alp said, not knowing what the term meant, but eager for relevant information.

"Average Daily Spread: 574–92. Peak Spread: 1,029–395. Overall graph—"

"Wait!" Alp cried. "I don't understand that! What do the figures mean?"

"The figures mean that your performance was successful."

"I mean what do they stand for? This 'Daily Spread'— where does it spread *from*, where does it go? I think I need the beginner's indoctrination."

The Game Machine obliged: "The Game is both a participant and a spectator sport, aside from its basic purpose: the instruction of history in a nonliterate society. The ratio of spectators to participants is approximately 1,000 to one. However, at any given moment only two or three students are watching any given player, on the average, because of the time required by other Galactic pursuits. In the course of a typical day approximately one hundred viewers will survey that part, however briefly. Accordingly, the standard spread comprises the survey figure together with the steady viewing figure: 100–2.5. For popular parts this rises—"

"Wait!" Alp cried again. "Do you mean people have been *watching* me?"

"Correct."

"They can tune in on me—the way I call another player on the screen? Only I can't see them?"

"Correct."

"Every moment of the whole part—two-and-a-half people were watching me, listening to me?"

"Incorrect. That is the standard spread. Your personal figures differ, as shown by your Audience Quotient."

Alp pondered this. He had had no idea he was being watched! Other players must have known the system, however, and been restrained by it. Perhaps his ignorance had even contributed to his success.

No, that wasn't right. Uga and Pei-li would never have gone along with the search for the document . . . "If the Galactics know about this, why—?"

"They do not know when participating. That aspect is blocked from their awareness for the duration of each part. This is to prevent players from being unduly influenced by the knowledge and playing incorrectly."

That made sense. Uga had been as ignorant as Alp, despite his seeming knowledge. "Would you give me my own figures again, please? With a running explanation, even if I am going to forget it all the moment I enter a new part!"

"You will remember it when the next part terminates," the Machine said. "Your average Daily Spread was 574–92. This means that on a typical day you were surveyed by 574 spectators, while 92 watched you at any given moment. A favorable Spectation ratio."

"Not two-and-a-half watching me all the time, but ninety-two," Alp said, musingly. "What was so interesting about me?"

"The manner in which you dealt with Uga at the outset. He was a player of some competence, yet you managed favorable terms. This alerted the viewers to your potential, and you picked up a number of fanatics."

"Fanatics? What are they?"

"Enthusiasts who follow a particular part exclusively, watching it for many hours a day. The number of such fans a given player accumulates is another indication of the depth of his popular appeal. Your total increased steadily to 105 by the time your part terminated.''

''A hundred-and-five? But if only ninety-two were watching—''

''You still do not understand the basic mathematics. Even fans must sleep, if nothing else. Normally it requires four or five fans to maintain a steady figure of one. Your 105 fans constituted only 22 steady watchers, statistically. The rest were partial fans and random viewers. Also, we are speaking of averages; the actual figures are variable—''

''That's enough,'' Alp said. ''Mathematics is not my strong point. When was this 'peak' you mentioned? I mean, when in the Game?''

''Your peak spread of 1,029–395 was achieved during your dialogue with Kokachin; this fell off sharply when she left the Game.''

''Why? What did they expect?'' That episode still hurt; Alp had held himself aloof from emotional concerns of the male-female type but had been vulnerable to that childish innocence.

''Spectators are notably lascivious in their tastes.''

''A nine-year-old girl? She would not be marriageable for three or four years.''

''Many things happen in the course of the Games that would not be legitimate in normal society, though the Galactic is more liberal than that you have known.''

Something about that statement alarmed him, so Alp smiled disarmingly. ''Because they think of it as a primitive situation . . . and don't realize they're being watched . . .'' Then

161

something else occurred to him. "If people are watching all the time—you must be watching too. To put them in touch."

"The Game Machine necessarily keeps track of all players," it agreed.

"Then you know—" Alp halted. *Did* it know about the document?

"The Game Machine maintains a complete record."

"Then why didn't you stop—?"

"The Game Machine does not interfere with individual parts so long as they are played within specification and no complaints are lodged."

Which was one difference between Machine and man! "None of the spectators complained?"

"None. They appreciate illicit excitement of any type. Your spread had a secondary peak at the time you appear to be considering of 988–450—an unusual ratio."

Interesting the way the Machine never referred to itself as "I" or jumped to a conclusion. It seemed truly neutral. Meanwhile, Alp found he understood the ratio. It meant that about one of every two people who surveyed him in that period stayed to watch steadily, skipping meals and sleep if need be. Complain? Not if that meant the termination of their vicarious lawbreaking! He had known the type in life . . .

"But the police," he said. "Why didn't *they* catch me when they had the chance?"

"Cross references between citizens and players are not routinely provided by the Game Machine, as this is deemed a legal invasion of privacy. The police were not at that time aware of your identity."

Invasion of privacy! Galactics didn't seem to mind having

their most intimate personal acts in the Game exposed to public view . . . yet balked at having their Galactic identities known. What a demonic set of values!

Alp shook his head. Neither Machine nor Galactic logic was his own—but he suspected that the Game Machine was tacitly collaborating as much as those spectators who had known he was breaking the rules, yet concealed that fact from the authorities. Why should the Machine assist him in such indirect yet effective manner?

He decided not to ask.

Chapter 13

TEMUJIN

Alp entered a minor Khitan part, reserving most of his credit for future emergencies. No sign of Khitan dominance appeared, and there were no characters named Jenghiz or Tatatunga. He lost track of Uga and Pei-li; as the Machine had explained, cross-references were not routinely provided, and the scope of the Game was wide.

The role terminated in 890 with a small positive balance, bringing Alp's cumulative score to 758 points. He entered another Khitan part—but the Khitans remained unimportant, and when it ended in 915 he had taken a loss, reducing his total to only 321 points. Still it was the barbarian Kirghiz, not the Khitan, who controlled the old Uigur territory. The higher standard of living the Uigurs had sponsored was now regressing, and more barbarians were filling in. Despairingly, Alp invested once more in the Khitans, spending the last of his credit for a soldier's role: in war there could be quick promotion—or quicker death.

T'ang had had his day. He lost his head about Day 900 and was ill. But the small giant Khitan now expanded into the power-vacuum. After 920 he drove Kirghiz back into the northern range and kept expanding.

Alp, a general in the conquering Khitan army, retired from his part in 950 with 1514 points. Several following good Khitan parts brought his total to over 5,000 points. But where was Jenghiz?

Then the current Chinese giant, Sung, made a deal with the barbarian Jurchid, of the Tungus family of nomads, and together they destroyed Khitan about 1123.

The historic document had betrayed him: the Khitans had dominated Steppe for two centuries but had never produced an extraordinary conquerer. Civilized and soft, as the Uigurs had been, they fell to intrigue and barbarism. Alp took a loss, and knew that Uga and Pei-li had suffered similarly.

Alp took two Sung parts, merely hanging on to his points while watching the situation. At length a new barbarian nomad began making motion: another Mongol.

The document had been genuine; Alp was sure of that. And the Game Machine was keeping history in line. Alp considered the situation again—and realized belatedly that though the Khitans were of the Mongol family, and that Jenghiz Qan was listed as a Mongol, he was not necessarily a Khitan. There were other, if minor, Mongol tribes in Steppe— and these were the same that were now joining the general stir to the north.

Should he take another safe Sung part—or gamble again

among the nomads? His mind urged the safe course—but his blood prevailed. Maybe he was misreading conditions—but this could be the situation he had been searching for all these centuries.

"Your choice of tribe?" the voice of the Game Machine inquired.

"Mongol," Alp said. "Chief level."

"Few parts of that specification are currently available," the Machine said. "If you will consider a chief in one of the related nations—Naiman, Kerayit, Markit—"

"No. Only Mongol."

"One thousand points entry fee."

"Subtract it from my account."

"As you wish." The Machine listed several Mongol chiefs for the Game year 1175. None were named Jenghiz.

Alp flexed his muscles restlessly. "I will wait," he said at last.

The booth became silent as the Machine's presence left. The Machine did not need to inform him that he had forfeited his entrance fee by declining all offerings. This was now a necessary expense. Alp still had a little over two thousand points. If the Jenghiz part did not open up soon, he would have to take something else. His nomad feel for power told him that this was his chance to land a really major part, and so he was gambling everything on that. He could wait up to five days before finally deciding; then he would have to take a part, or leave the Game entirely.

How was Uga doing? The two had met now and again in the course of the Khitan history, with Uga generally doing better because of his ability to buy superior parts. Was Uga also now waiting in a booth for Jenghiz to appear?

Alp sat it out as long as he could bear—three days—then made a second application. Game time was now 1178.

As he entered the booth, he had a bright notion. "I should like to consider Mongol chiefs and Uigur scholars," he said.

The Machine accepted his fee and displayed a wide range of Uigur scholars. They were in small demand because of the prevailing illiteracy, so their entry fee was smaller—but he had to pay the full chief fee if he wanted to look at both. This was cheaper than paying two separate fees to check them one at a time, since he didn't really want a Uigur part.

There were over a hundred identities available. Alp checked each doggedly and paid close attention to each description. And suddenly he found it: Tata-tunga!

Now he was certain this was the age of Jenghiz Qan. Jenghiz and Tata-tunga were contemporaries. His heart pounding, he asked to see the Mongols.

They were now reduced to two; other players had snapped up the others, and new ones had not developed apace. Experienced Game players were quick to note new trends, and there was a lot of potential in the new Mongols should they ever become unified.

Neither was Jenghiz. "I will wait," Alp said again, regretfully. Had someone else already taken the part—or was it yet to come? If so, would it show within his time limit?

He waited one more day. His deadline, both in time and points, was near. This was it.

He applied the third time, in 1179, and paid his fee. Now

there were two new parts—and neither was Jenghiz. He had lost.

Faced with that fatal prospect, Alp had a sudden inspiration. Jenghiz could be a *title*, not a name! One of the other parts, correctly played, could *become* Jenghiz! That threw the whole thing open again!

The parts offered were Jamuqa and Temujin. Alp considered them carefully. The first was a man of the Jajirat tribe of the Mongols, barely fourteen years old but technically a chief. The second was even younger, twelve or thirteen, the son of a powerful chief who had just died, Yesugei. Unfortunately that chief had also had powerful enemies—who now were the enemies of the child. That did not augur well!

The older boy, Jamuqa, was obviously the better choice. But Alp had struggled along for several parts and learned that often the least likely prospect had the best actual potential. Why not gamble all the way?

No—he had to trust his judgment, though it might be flawed. He would start from the better base and work to make it become what—

"Deletion," the Machine said. "The part of Jamuqa has just been taken. Will you consider the remaining one or go to another tribe?"

Alp sighed. Even as he dawdled here, other players in other booths were moving in, making faster decisions. "I will accept Temujin," he said with resignation.

Alp sat silently in his *ger*. Just a few minutes ago, Game time, his Game-father Yesugei had been treacherously poisoned at a banquet by the Tatars of the east. Now he was

169

Temujin, barely thirteen years old, the nominal heir to the leadership of the Kiyat clan of the Mongols—already deserted by two-thirds of its membership. Who would trust the leadership of a mere boy?

And he *was* a boy. The Machine had applied makeup that made him seem youthful and slender, and the Machine had drawn away some of his manly strength. In a few days these handicaps would fade, and he would be himself again; but right now his resources were those of the age he represented. It was an amazing transformation, and not one he liked.

Temujin's mother, Oelun-eke, was an energetic woman. She was to have been the wife of a chief of the Markit, for she was beautiful; but Yesugei had abducted her on her nuptial night and married her himself. The Markit had been vengeance-minded for some time thereafter, and they were formidable fighters—but Yesugei had been too strong in his home region. He had assumed the chiefship not only of the minor Kiyat clan, but of the powerful Borjigin tribe of Mongols. As such, he had been a natural leader among all the Mongol clans and tribes. Now that he was dead, there could be renewed trouble from the Markit.

Meanwhile, Oelun's concern was for the safety of her children. She struggled valiantly to salvage what she could of her eldest son's heritage, carrying the banner of the nine yak-tails from one Kiyat family to another, pleading for their return. But it was useless. Only Munlik, the confidential adviser to Chief Yesugei and his wife, remained loyal. The Kiyat clan had been fragmented by the death of its leader—and how could a newly-orphaned child hope to bring it back together?

Alp had been in difficult situations before and had no intention of letting Temujin's potential go to waste. The boy, though young, had specifications that made him smart and strong—as smart and strong as Alp had been at that age, by no coincidence. If he could prove himself among the Mongols—and Alp's Turkish pride made him certain that he could!—many of the deserting tribesmen would remember their faltering loyalty and return. Temujin would not remain thirteen indefinitely; if he survived to full manhood, he could be physically and politically powerful.

The time to act was now. Theoretically he was overcome by grief for his father, so that it was his mother who had to rally the tribe—but that was not the aspect of his new part he cared to stress. Alp touched the button of the intercom. "Munlik!" he called.

There was a long pause, but finally the Mongol's face appeared on the screen. "Yes, Temujin, my boy?"

"Yes *chief*!" Alp snapped. "Report to my *ger* at once for conference."

Munlik looked weary. He was an older man who might once have been physically strong; now his face was sallow and lined. He wore his dark hair in the Mongol tonsure, with a strip three fingers wide shaved from ear to ear and a crescent-shaped fringe covering his forehead to the eyebrows. The rest of his hair was gathered up and braided down the back, as was Alp's own. "Son, I have seven boys of my own to look out for, and no wife to tend them. The clan is done for. You'll survive longer if you accept reality and drop your pretensions."

Alp suppressed the sudden fury he felt at this insolence.

171

Munlik's advice would have been well-taken—for an ordinary player. There was scant profit in taking a losing part too seriously. But Alp was driven by more than player success. This was his major chance to win the tremendous stake he needed to preserve his Galactic identity beyond the Game of Steppe. Failure meant the end—of everything. A long-lived but indifferent part was worthless; he would achieve greatness in the Game, or die—in life as in history. Let this sycophant Munlik beware!

"My father was chief," Alp said with all the even authority of his thirteen years. It no longer seemed as if he were animating a part; he really felt it! "I am his eldest son. The Kiyat clan is strong enough—if it only stays together."

"So your attractive mother tells me," Munlik said tolerantly.

That was no better. Oelun's beauty was the envy of lesser tribeswomen, and the boy Temujin was the first to know it. This bastard already had his eye on the fair widow! "You and I are going to keep it together," Alp said. "You say you have a family of seven to look out for—do you think *I* don't? Five brothers, two sisters—and a mother."

Munlik studied him a moment. Alp had tacitly served notice that permission would not be forthcoming from the new head of the family for whatever designs the man might have on Oelun. Not unless he obeyed Temujin implicitly. "You leave me little choice," Munlik said sadly. "I must seek sanctuary with a functioning and hospitable tribe."

So now the man was threatening to desert him too, thinking Alp would have to capitulate. "Munlik, you swore to serve me as you did my father, when you sought me out among the Qongirat a few days ago!'' Ten minutes ago, Game time—but it was the same.

"And so I do, Temujin, in the best fashion I know. When I spoke to you then, I had to put up a proper front before the Qongirat chief, whose pretty little daughter you so recently betrothed. But now I perceive that the situation of the Kiyat clan is hopeless, so I serve you by making you understand this at the outset.'' His voice became gentle: the tone of one who knows best. "Do as I do, Temujin—enlist with an intact clan, for your own safety and that of your family. Perhaps the Qongirat—they should succor you for the sake of young Borte. Or go to Togrul the Kerayit, who owes your father a blood-debt. This course at least will offer you some protection from your many enemies.''

"Enemies? Like the dour Markit?'' Alp said contemptuously, though his older Uigur mind knew this was bravado. "They are far away!''

"I mean the Tays, lad: the Tayichiut clan. Chief Targhutai Kiriltug and his brother have laid claim to the chiefship of the entire Borjigin tribe, now that your father is dead. Targ means to kill you, and is even now assembling his warriors for that task. As long as you live, his claim is insecure, for that position is nominally yours now.''

A valid warning. Targ had good reason to eliminate his young rival! But the boyish temper would not heed. "So you're running out!''

"Temujin, I would be doing you a fatal disservice if I encouraged you to stand and fight. Targ can mass ten thousand horse, and the best you can do now is two or three hundred.''

173

"Then get out!" Alp shouted. "I have no use for cowards!"

Munlik did not deign to answer this slur. He was no coward, and Alp knew it; he was a cautious, pragmatic player who had held his part for a long time and was now taking the sensible course. Young Temujin's position *was* virtually hopeless.

The screen faded. Immediately Alp called his Mongol mother. The lovely, freshly-careworn face appeared, and he wondered momentarily who played that part. She was well cast!

"Munlik's pulling out," Alp said.

She sighed. "Temujin, I tried. But now we are alone. Are you sure it wouldn't be better to—"

"No! We'll get along on our own. We'll forage here in our home territory until . . ." He trailed off, but she understood him. *Until he was a man.*

But the tiny family group was not granted much respite. In a few Minutes a hostile fleet appeared in the sky, and the markings were Tay. Targ was coming to ensure the demise of his rival claimant to the chiefship of the larger Mongol tribe. Some five hundred ships.

There was only one thing to do. Alp alerted his five brothers, packed his mother and sisters aboard three of their crafts, and took off. The six ships, representing all the remaining horses of the Kiyat clan, fled to the Kentei Mountains.

The mountains of Kentei were stellar red giants whose huge gravity wells made rapid travel difficult. They were not extensive by Galactic standards, but they were suitably obscured by surrounding debris to make the vicinity an excellent hiding place.

Targ's ships pursued for some distance. They could have caught some of the fugitives readily enough, but Targ preferred to tease his prey a little, a wolf tossing a live but crippled mouse in the air. Alp gritted his teeth with fury even though his double-loaded steeds desperately needed the respite Targ's sport provided.

"Qasar," Alp said to his younger brother. "You're the best shot with the bow. Try to distract them."

Qasar obediently decelerated and was lost to screen contact. The arrows fired by Targ's posse stopped passing so near, and that was a good sign. Qasar, only eleven, was already a master bowman. Even grown warriors did not make fun of his prowess . . . long. He had killer aim—and killer nerve.

Alp, satisfied that they had lost their pursuit, established an orbit close to a large dim star and formed the three double-loaded horses into a cluster. They were short of supplies and their mounts were fatigued; this merged orbit would conserve fuel and make the drifting vessels almost impossible to spot. Targ would be looking for them on some depot planet, not in space!

Alp left the younger boys with the women while he made a drive for one of those Game supply depots. Qasar was still out of touch somewhere in space, so Alp took his twelve-year-old half-brother Bekter to cover for him on that lightning raid. He had never gotten along well with this child of his father's concubine, but this was no time for quibbles.

They were successful. They landed, loaded, and took off

before Targ's guards realized who they were. In minutes they were back in the Kentei region of space. "Now cruise in easy," Alp warned. "They may be watching us, and we don't want to give away our hideout."

"Cruise in yourself," Bekter said sharply. "This stuff'll last me long enough to make it to Naiman space!"

His own brother had turned traitor already! Now Alp could not afford to trust him, for Bekter knew where the orbit was and might use that information to buy his own freedom if he were captured by Targ.

"Qasar!" Alp snapped on the open channel. This would be audible to anyone else in nearby space, but this was an emergency.

"Here!" Qasar replied, the scant time lag showing that he was not far off, fortunately. Communications were limited to lightspeed, even when the ships were traveling at light multiples; Alp didn't understand this but wasn't concerned. It was good to be back in touch with his stout brother—and he needed him now!

"Bekter is stealing our supplies. You know what to do." Qasar didn't like Bekter either.

"Now just a minute!" Bekter cried, alarmed. "It's no big deal! You can get more—"

"And get cut down by Targ!" Qasar retorted angrily.

Then Alp fired from one angle, and Qasar from another. Alp's arrow missed, but Qasar's hit. In a few seconds Bekter's ship went dead, and he was out of the Game.

It was a brutal penalty—but betrayal of one's family was the ultimate nomad crime. Turk and Mongol agreed on that!

Alp had no question about the loyalty of his full brothers,

Qasar, Qachiun and Temuge. But his other half-brother, Belgutai—how could he be certain of him, after this? Alp couldn't eliminate the child without cause, and certainly hoped it would not be necessary. But Belgutai would have to be watched most carefully. Any slip would finish them all!

Chapter 14

FRIENDS

In a few Hours they were low on supplies again, thanks to Bekter's defection. Single horses could not carry much, and Alp had not dared overload his own. Targ seemed to have given up active pursuit, however, probably assuming that Temujin had been washed out of the Game by now. Still, Alp was cautious. He went alone this time, and not to the same depot.

And dropped right into an ambush. As he stepped from his mount bowmen appeared all around him. Resistance would have meant instant stunning. He had after all been outsmarted.

Targ was a big coarse Mongol, gray-eyed like most of the true blood—sometimes called the league of gray-eyed men. He looked on Alp with affected contempt. Alp's eyes were gray enough, but his hair now had a reddish cast, suggesting Turk or even Indo-European ancestry. "So this is the mon-

179

grel stripling who pretends to be chief!'' But his revenge for
that impertinence could not be satisfied by mere elimination—
and he, like many players, was hesitant to wipe out another
part too directly outside of battle. If the Game Machine had
not scheduled that part for termination, the attempt might be
balked—costing the other party points. "Put him in the
cangue!''

They bound his hands and put the heavy pseudowood
collar that was the cangue over his head. Thus weighted and
confined, he was put on display as an object of ridicule
before all the Mongol players who came to the depot. Alp
knew that Targ would arrange a terminal accident for him
soon—as soon as it could be attempted privately, without
record, so as to conceal possible failure. Meanwhile, ridicule.

This was the part he had hoped to convert into that of the
presumed lord of the world: Jenghiz Qan! In less than a Day
he had run into termination. Munlik had been right: he had
been too ambitious and had only squandered his opportunity.
A part that deviated too radically from the historical script
was soon nullified.

Soon the guards drifted away, for attention spans were
short in the swiftly-changing events of the Game. Only one
remained to watch the prisoner. Alp dived for him, cracking
the heavy cangue into his head and knocking the man out in
an unusual fashion: by hand. How would the Machine evaluate
that?

Alp staggered out onto the surface of the planet, seeking
his horse. It was gone. In seconds Targ's men would be after
him, and this time they would not hesitate to stun him.

There was a large reservoir of water beside the station,

kept fresh by growing green plants and selected fish. He jumped into it and submerged all but his head. The Tay warriors charged along the shore, thinking he had run on by. He wanted to conceal himself entirely, but the solid collar was buoyant, and of course he had to breathe. If anyone looked directly at him, here in the reeds . . .

But Targ's men ran on, careless in their haste. Alp did not dare move, though the water was chill. The real Temujin would have been hardened to this sort of exploit, even as a boy—but Alp had grown just a bit soft in the course of his near-Year's participation in the Game. It had been almost three-hundred-and-fifty Days since the gorge! Civilization tended to corrupt manhood!

Another group of Mongols came, walking slowly. Three men, two young. Not Targ's ilk, but from another clan. A chief and his two sons, by the look of them—probably at the depot coincidentally. Everyone came to one depot or another, at one time or another, for supplies. Would they help a Kiyat in trouble?

The chief turned his head and looked directly at Alp. Their eyes met; then, without interrupting his conversation, the man turned away.

The chief had seen him, that was certain—but had neither exclaimed in surprise nor sounded the alarm. But also he had not offered to help. Did that mean he understood—but was staying out of it? Helping neither side? Or that he was sympathetic, but afraid to commit himself in the presence of Targ's troops?

The strange chief's ship was near. Alp watched the three go to it. No warriors were in sight. Soon the chief would mount his horse, and his sons theirs, and take off for their home parts. Alp scrambled out of the chill water and charged across the interval, banging his collar upon the chief's port.

It opened quickly and a wide-eyed youth stood there. It was not, after all, the chief's ship, but that of one of his boys. Alp was lucky he hadn't misjudged worse!

"What—?" the youth asked. He was younger than Alp, perhaps twelve.

"I am Temujin—son of Yesugei—chief of the Kiyat clan. Targ means to kill me! I beg your help!"

The boy hastened to fetch his father. "I am Sorqan-Shira, chief of the Sulda clan," the man said. "These are my sons, Chilaun whom you have just met and Chimbai." He looked nervously across the parking lot toward the depot building. "But this is none of our affair."

"It is *now*!" Alp cried, ducking down behind the ship so as to be less conspicuous. "You must help me—or leave me to die! Targ means to usurp my Borjigin title . . ."

Sorqan considered. "It is unwise to interfere with the schedules of the Game Machine—"

"Sire!" Chilaun cried. "He came to me begging succor! How could I ever call myself a man if I allow this? We must at least get him out of that cangue!"

Sorqan made his decision quickly once challenged, as befitted a Mongol chief shamed by his son. "Very well—we will free him and hide him from Targ. But no more than that. He must find his own way home. No man can say for certain what is in the mind of the Machine."

Chilaun got a welder and carefully angled the beam to burn into the collar while Alp stayed absolutely still. It was nervous business, but the boy's hand was marvelously steady. He would make a good fighter! "I have heard of your case," Chilaun remarked as he worked. "I do not like Targ."

Alp's neck was partially singed before the job was done, for there was no way to get the last of the cut made without touching; but he held steady and both cangue and manacles came off. Sorqan fed these into this ship's converter, destroying the evidence. But already Targ's men were passing from ship to ship in the lot, searching for the fugitive. The situation looked ugly, for the three Sulda clansmen could not hope to resist these troops.

"Into the wagon!" Sorqan cried. "And make no outcry whatever happens, for the smoke of my own fire will die out forever if they discover you here!"

Alp dived into their adjacent wagon: a ship designed for hauling supplies during long journeys. It was little more than a sealable shell that had to be hauled by regular horses, useless in battle. This one was filled with pseudowool for the nomad players' clothing, and the stuff was hot and scratchy on his soaking body.

He lay rigid, completely buried in the infernal stuff. Even breathing was hazardous, for the dust made him inclined to sneeze. He heard mutterings and Sorqan's resentful objection; then a paralysis beam probed the hold, as of a sword being thrust randomly through, and one leg went numb.

Had that blade touched a vital organ, he would have been finished then, to Targ's satisfaction. But Alp made no sound or motion.

After the warriors were gone, the two boys pulled him out. Chilaun loaned him his own horse, together with what supplies the ship could accommodate. "Targ has humiliated us by this search," Chilaun said grimly. "One day when I am a man I shall have an accounting!"

"Now get on home to your mother and brothers!" Sorqan said gruffly, relieved to be rid of him. But the test of the man was not in his words, and the measure of his two sons was not in their age.

"I will remember this," Alp said simply. "When my circumstance improves, and when you need help, send Chilaun to me!"

The orbit was vacant. Oelun-eke and her children were gone with their remaining ships. Alp knew she would not have deserted him. Had they been driven elsewhere by hunger—or had they been betrayed?

Alp searched the Kentei region, broadcasting his identity on the band he had used to locate Qasar. The odds were that they were gone from the Game, raided and dispatched while he was prisoner—but though he might actually fare better without them, he could not simply write them off. There were other loyalties besides success.

He found them at last, hungry, their horses exhausted and useless. They were in another orbit, ready to quit the Game themselves rather than seek help that could prejudice Temujin's own chances. "But why did you move?" Alp demanded.

"My responsibility," Qasar said. "I feared you had been captured and that Targ's ships would come—"

"You know I would never betray my family!" Alp exclaimed.

Qasar shook his head, thinking it out. He was a fine archer

184

but not bright otherwise. "That's what Belgutai said. He said you would return—that we should wait. But I thought they would trace us the same way they traced you—"

"Let it drop," Alp said tiredly. So Belgutai had been loyal!

After that things improved, marginally. The boys grew in size and cunning. Alp was amazed to see how even a few Hours made a difference, as the Machine conditioning faded and allowed the grown men to break free of the boyish cocoons. Qasar developed into a big, broad-shouldered man, and Alp's oldest sister became a buxom woman.

Heartened by the maturing power of his little band, Alp left the sanctuary of the mountains on occasion to make his survival known to his former Kiyat clansmen, and formally demand the chieftain's tithe that was due him. He had little success, but that was not the main point. The idea was to let them know what their obligations were and keep reminding them of an increasingly viable alternative. The young man of fourteen was more formidable than the lad of thirteen . . . but not yet enough to reclaim his clan.

Still, he acquired several more ships, until he had nine of his own: enough to mount every member of his party including the girls, with one to spare. Targ's warriors no longer prowled in the vicinity; it was too dangerous for small parties and not worth the effort of a large party. Besides, Targ had pretty well consolidated his claim on the Borjigin tribe, so Alp was less of a threat. Alp and Qasar were now able to restock openly at the depots, though they always kept one ship in orbit . . . just in case.

When Temujin was fifteen, eight of their ships were stolen. They emerged from the supply complex to see them taking off, on slave-circuit to a group of Tay raiders. More mischief by Targ's men!

Belgutai had the ninth horse in orbit. Quickly he landed—but his lone mount could not carry them all. "I'll go after them!" he volunteered.

"You couldn't handle it," Qasar said. "I'll take your horse and go."

"You'd have no chance either," Alp said. "I'll have to do it myself." He was not the best bowshot, but he was certainly the most cunning fighter of the family group, so this was reasonable. Without those horses they would be confined to the planet, prey to Targ's men.

He left them at the depot, a precarious location but necessary for now. The chase was difficult, for the raiders were better fueled and provisioned than he. He was barely able to keep track of their traces. After fifteen Minutes he was afraid his horse would fail, forcing him to give up. Then he spied a strange ship.

It was chancy but necessary. He hailed it on his screen. "I am Temujin, chief of the Kiyat. I seek no quarrel with you."

"I am Borchu of the Arulat," the other replied immediately. His face on the screen seemed about Alp's own Game-age. "What do you wish?"

Alp recognized the name: this was the son of another clan chief. This lad could help him—if he chose. "I need a fresh steed, quickly. I have little but promises to offer in return."

Borchu considered. "I have heard the word of Yesugei was good. Not so, that of his enemies."

So the Arulat would help! "Word-breaking is hideous in a ruler," Alp said sincerely. "Eight horses of mine have been stolen. Help me, and half are yours."

"Good enough! I will ride with you."

Borchu gave him a remount, and the two of them set out in fresh pursuit of the bandits. In another fifteen Minutes they caught up.

The Tays had landed on another depot planet, satisfied that they had easily outrun the pursuit. How far could one lad get on a tired horse? The eight ships were parked in the lot, unguarded, while the thieves caroused inside.

It was a simple matter to transfer the reins of the slave circuits and lead the eight away. Alp was reminded of the time, back in his very first part, when the T'ang Chinese had slipped the reins of the Uigur delegation's spare horses.

But Targ's warriors were not entirely napping. In seconds half a dozen of their ships were spaceborne and in hot pursuit. The Tay leader's steed was fresh and swift, and possessed a lariat: a ship-anchored cannon whose shells were magnetic, capable of latching on to a fleeing ship and nullifying its drive, making it easy prey for stunner or tractor beam. The range of the lariat was short—but the enemy was steadily gaining and would soon be near enough.

"Lend me your bow," Borchu said to Temujin. "I'll drop back and shoot him down."

This was a polite figurative way to put it; of course Borchu had his own. He was merely clearing his proposed course of action with his new friend.

"The others might catch up and wound you," Alp said generously, for he rather liked this man's attitude. "I'll do it

myself.'' He looped about, aimed, and loosed an arrow at the
Tay horseman. It scored, and the ship went dead. The others
reined in as they came up to it. Alp's talents were improving!
The threat was over.

"You're mighty handy with that bow!'' Borchu said
admiringly.

"My brother Qasar is better.''

"Come and meet my father,'' Borchu urged. "I know he
will like you!''

"I have to get back to my family. My mother and brothers
are dependent on me. Take your four horses and depart with
my gratitude; without your help I would have had nothing.''

"I don't want the ships!'' Borchu protested. "If I take
what is yours, how could you call me comrade? Come home
with me and tell your tale, and afterwards I shall ride with
you and be your officer.''

Alp was deeply flattered by this unexpected offer and
determined that Borchu should never in his life regret it.
"You will be my general!'' he exclaimed, and the bargain
was struck.

Chapter 15

BORTE

The three strong arms of Temujin, Qasar and Borchu, supported by the younger brothers and a dozen ships, made the nucleus of the Kiyat clan credible at last. The wandering clansmen began to drift back, and more of them now yielded tithes. Old Munlik himself returned. Alp did not like him but had to accept him—and the presence of the man's seven strong sons added considerably to the clan's power. No one laughed, now, at Alp's pretensions of leadership. The tide of his Mongol fortune had turned.

He did not fool himself that he was anywhere near the success he required, however. All he had done was to survive and grow into manhood, and make the role viable. He remained the young chief of a minor clan: one among many.

When Temujin was seventeen years old—four Days after Alp assumed the part—he called upon the chief of the Qongirat

Mongols. This was another necessary step in his ascension, whatever his personal feelings.

His three hundred ships suddenly landed at the Qongirat home world, alarming the natives. Frantically they mustered their defensive forces.

"Peace!" Alp called as Chief Dai-Sechen's worried face appeared on his screen. "I am Temujin—and I come to beg the hand of your lovely daughter!"

The old man's face broke into a relieved smile. "Welcome, Temujin of the Kiyat! I had not expected to see you thus alive!"

The girl Borte had been just nine years old when Temujin and Yesugei had visited here last, just prior to Alp's assumption of his role. Temujin, historically, had seen the pretty child and asked for her in marriage, and Dai-Sechen had been pleased to agree. Such a link with powerful Yesugei, Chief of the Kiyat and the important Borjigin tribe, had been an attractive prospect. But almost immediately thereafter, Yesugei had been poisoned by the treacherous Tatars. Temujin had been visiting here when Munlik came to fetch him with the awful news.

Thus there was important history in this betrothal—but Alp himself had never seen the girl. He had no great expectations—there was no certainty that a pretty child would make a beautiful woman—but now the fortunes of the clans had been reversed, and it was Temujin who needed the alliance, not the Qongirat. So he had come to do his duty: a child-wife was not after all too great a price to pay for success!

He had a surprise coming! Borte had waited for Days for his coming, and now she was no child of nine but a woman

of thirteen—and lovely. She wore a long dress of white felt,
with a headdress of pseudo-birch bark covered with precious
silk, and the black braids of her hair were entwined with
silver coins and tiny statues. Her nose was small, her eyes
bright, and she had an elegance of bearing far beyond her
years.

Alp knew it was only a part. But there was something
special about her. He saw before him a girl who could have
been a true Mongol princess—or even the wife of a Uigur
Khagan! Surely the actress had the blood of the historical
Steppe in her. Possession of this one would be a delight!

Dai-Sechen threw a gala wedding party. Alp and his retinue ate until stuffed. No need now to worry about poison;
these were Qongirat allies, not Tatar enemies! Then Temujin
took off after his bride-to-be, in the time-honored ceremony
of the Steppe.

"You!" he cried suddenly, as if he had just for the first
time realized that there was a woman present. He advanced
on pretty Borte while the merrymakers chuckled.

The girl screamed fetchingly and fled from the tent. Alp
chased her out onto the surface of the planet, burdened by his
monstrous meal and much fine Steppe liquor. She skipped
lightly into her own tent, and he lurched after.

Her sisters and handmaidens lay in ambush inside. They
flung themselves on him, and he struggled drunkenly to
throw them off and win through to Borte. There was rather
pleasant contact of bodies, for these girls were young and
healthy and he was not as intoxicated as he pretended; some
of the screams were genuine. At last he threw them off and
grabbed his bride by her slender waist; she was now laughing

too hard to resist. He threw her over his shoulder and bore her triumphantly toward his horse, while her sisters wailed amid their declining chuckles.

Borte, full-bodied but lithe as a wildcat, halted her supposed struggle for a moment. "You're a strong one!" she murmured in his ear. "Do you exercise regularly?"

Déjà-vu: the feeling of having been through this before. "You'll find out!" he muttered, swinging her aboard.

"Are you sorry you betrothed a nine-year-old child?" she inquired mischievously.

He slapped her on her woman's bottom as he set her down. "It is the sacrifice I make for history," he said, appraising her afresh. She was no child now! "Anyway, that was four years ago."

"More like four *centuries* ago!" she said, giving him the direct eye. "Don't you remember?"

Alp's brain seemed to spin within his skull. "Koka!"

"That was one part," she admitted. "Kokachin, imitation princess. I had thought it might lead me to adventure, and it did—but more than that, it showed me a man. I have been trying to catch up with you ever since—and I finally made it! Cost me a pretty fee to play opposite you . . ."

"But you really *were* a child! How—?"

"I was no child, Ko-lo! Haven't you observed the Machine's makeup abilities?"

He had indeed. He had just never thought to make this particular connection! So the Chinese mock-princess really would have grown to womanhood in four days—had she survived the part! "When I get you to my *ger*," he promised her seriously, "we shall begin catching up on those four centuries!"

But there was a brief delay while they loaded her dowry, a precious pseudosable cloak. Then Alp and his party took off for home. It had been a successful mission! He only regretted that there was not space enough, riding double on his horse, to commence that four-century makeup. He was able only to snatch a handful of promise.

The most powerful ruler of the contemporary Steppe was Togrul, lord of the Kerayit. Alp took a small party and some gifts—including Borte's dowry of sable—and paid a diplomatic call on Togrul at his major planet of Karakorum. This did not match the sophistication of the great Chinese residences but was far more civilized than anything most Mongols knew.

Togrul was a man of Yesugei's generation, confident in his power. He could muster fifty thousand ships from his own dominions, and more if he drew on his dependencies and alliances. Temujin's forces were pitiful in comparison, yet Alp was not abashed.

"What brings you here, nephew?" Togrul demanded genially.

And Alp had his second recent shock of recognition. "Uga!" he exclaimed.

"Play the part, Alp!" the man muttered, glancing at his retainers nearby.

Alp played the part. "I merely wanted to renew acquaintance," he said, and there was now a double meaning.

"Need help, eh?"

193

"No, I thought I'd offer you mine."

Togrul laughed and put his arm around Alp's shoulders. "You're as sharp as your father was! I don't mind admitting, son, Yesugei helped me out of a pinch once. Some fine fighting men in that Borjigin tribe of his! I'm not forgetful what I owe him, even if he's dead now. Why didn't you come to me before?"

"Didn't have enough of a clan," Alp admitted. And of course he hadn't known this part would be played by his old friend and collaborator Uga!

"Son, didn't you know I'd have helped you in an instant, for the sake of your father? You didn't have to take any guff off an impostor like Targ!"

Alp shrugged. "I just like to do things my own way, beholden to none." But that wasn't true; he had debts to Chilaun, who had now joined him for experience, and to Borchu, now his leading lieutenant, and to many others who had befriended him similarly in need. But they accepted his command; Togrul was hardly of that level!

"Son, you're damn lucky you got out of that cangue! Take my advice: next time you get in a bind, don't fool around with individual heroism! Call on me! And when *I'm* in a bind, I'll call on *you!*"

They both laughed—but the alliance was no joke. Alp had now become a client of the Kerayit leader, and when Togrul made war, Alp could be called to contribute his resources and perhaps his life. He had waited until now so that he could make the alliance honorably, retaining a large measure of independence. His experiences in the Kentei mountains had shown him that in this part more than any other he survived only by luck and sufferance—and he could not afford to depend on either indefinitely. So it was time for well-chosen compacts.

They entered Togrul's private chambers. "Glad to see you, Alp!" Uga cried. "We're finally at the Mongol times! But I thought you'd have a better part!"

"I was looking for Jenghiz," Alp said. "But I realized—"

"You know, it came to me that Jenghiz is only a title, a dynasty name! Any leader could fill it, if he had a proper power base. That's why I bought into this one."

"You—Jenghiz Qan?" Alp asked, surprised.

"Not yet! But in a few years, why not? I'm not a Mongol—but I have Mongol clients! I could conquer every remaining Mongol tribe tomorrow, if I chose! But that would complicate the picture unnecessarily and get me embroiled in debilitating rivalries. No percentage in that! So when the time comes, I'll simply declare myself a Mongol and assume the title."

"But I—"

"But you expected to take Jenghiz yourself. I know. But I looked at it this way: if you got it, fine. But what if you *didn't*? Should it go by accident to some dumb player we never heard of? Best thing I could do was go for it myself. I came on this scene at a different time than you did, and parts move fast, so I'm not even competing with you."

"Yes . . . of course," Alp agreed. It did make sense. Every player had to strive for the best he could do . . . and he really doubted that Kerayit part could assume Mongol status like that. Meanwhile, he did have a stout ally in Uga, who seemed to have picked up in this part where he had left off as Khagan of the Uigurs, and who was the one man in all the Game who really understood him.

It was all part of the Game . . . but Alp could not help himself. He was in love with Borte, player and part. The Game-romance that had started in 841 was a real romance in the late twelfth century, 1184.

"But it passes so quickly!" he complained after making furious love.

"Do it again and it will be much slower," she promised him.

"I mean our marriage. I shall hardly have tested you before you become an old woman!"

"But what a way to grow old!" she said, laughing. "And there will be other parts for both of us . . ."

"All too short! Koka, when the Game is over, will you—"

She waited expectantly—but he could not say what they both wanted him to say. For his Galactic life was dependent on his Game life; if he did not do extremely well here, there would be no future at all for him. How could he ask her to share that risk? He hadn't even told her of it.

"Yes I will!" she said. "I don't care what you are in real life, or how well you do in Steppe, or what you look like. You told me before that you weren't married—"

"I'm not," he said quickly. "But there is something you should know before you decide. I—"

"I decided four centuries ago," she said. "Then, now, and forever!"

"But I may not even have any existence outside the—"

His voice was drowned out by the sound of a ship landing

almost on top of the *ger*. Alp, naked, charged out, his sword flashing. "You crazy fool!" he bawled in good Galactic slang. "This is the camping area!"

But ships were landing all about, and warriors were dismounting, fully dressed and armed. They were not his men. This was a raiding party!

Alp fought, but there were too many of them, and his own warriors were not organized.

There was a scream behind him. "Temujin!"

Nude Borte was being dragged away by two of the enemy. Half a dozen more warriors stood between them. Alp's own men were all occupied.

Alp charged back toward the tent, laying out warriors right and left. They were Game-players, not true nomads: no match for him individually. He was an energumen with the sword. But there were so many! And more ships were landing!

In moments his own horse would be stolen. Then he would be truly helpless! He could not reach Borte, who was already being hauled into an enemy vessel. It was a heart-wrenching decision—the same he had made back in life when his wife and child were killed—but the only one; he turned and ran for his steed.

Even then, it was close. Had he not been bred to the Steppe, he would not have made it. He lost count of the warriors he downed in that mad scramble. But the same chaos that prevented him from saving his wife also inhibited the enemy from reacting to his new thrust. He made it.

He was not out of it yet! A dozen ships rose with him. For the first time he saw their markings: Markit.

Markit—the toughest individual fighters of the region. Suddenly he understood. Oelun-eke, mother of Temujin, had been stolen from a Markit chief. It had taken eighteen Days for the Markit revenge to materialize—but the time had been well chosen! Now Temujin's own bride had been stolen in a similar manner!

There was a certain justice to it that Alp would have admired at another time. Someone among the Markit was a very shrewd player—and the Game Machine would give that man bonus points for that initiative and planning and nicety of execution! Perhaps Alp's own life had been spared intentionally, so that the precise point of the raid would be manifest, in case the Machine had any doubt.

Beautiful—but they had made one little mistake. They had not taken into account the possibility that the player of the role of Temujin the Kiyat would actually fall in love with the player of Borte the Qongirat, and would go to extraordinary measures to recover her—Game or no Game.

The real Temujin had had stern pride; Alp knew that, just from the nature of the part. He doubted, now, that Temujin was the one scheduled to become Jenghiz Qan; the boy had the proper qualities, but the elements of the Game were too heavily weighted against him. He would already have been eliminated more than once had not Alp bent the part just enough to gain essential help. Still, it was a decent part—and he was about to stretch it to its limits.

Let the Game Machine stop him openly, if it had to! Life no longer had meaning without Koka/Borte, and nothing but death would balk him!

Meanwhile, he had to elude his pursuers. This turned out to be easier than it might have been. Qasar and Borchu had escaped the planet, together with a number of his men. Also, he had posted several ships in orbit. They had not been able to stop the abrupt surprise attack but had evidently given a good account of themselves, and a number survived. These stray forces now closed in and provided cover for his escape. It was a rout, certainly—but they made it safely to the familiar Kentei range.

Alp did not stay in hiding. The real Temujin might have licked his wounds fatalistically and taken a new wife, but Alp's needs were different and his pride more devious. The moment the enemy cleared out, he took a new steed and went to Togrul the Kerayit. He also sent Borchu and Qasar and Chilaun out to make contact with other Mongol clans, in the hope that some would make common cause with him on this mission. Obviously the Markit would not settle for one prisoner when there was other loot to be taken, and it behooved other Mongols to drive the common enemy out. But of course he wanted more than that; he meant to invade the Markit homespace itself, and that would be no mean undertaking!

Togrul came through with a small army and led it personally. He seemed eager to discharge his debt to Temujin's father. Alp hoped it would not be too obvious that he and Uga were private friends. By Game logic, now that Alp had cashed in this asset, he should not be able to depend on further help from the Kerayit at a later date, should another emergency arise. That was the seeming foolishness of this mission: he was not doing it for anything important, like vengeance for insult or acquisition of a throne. Just for the recovery of one wife, whose value would surely have been decreased by the uses to which the Markit men would put her in the interim.

Well, perhaps he would not have to ask for help another time. He hoped so!

One of the other Mongol clans did respond. Jamuqa, the young chief of the Jajirat, arrived with a welcome complement. Together, the Kiyat, Jajirat and Kerayit elements made a formidable fleet.

Alp welcomed Jamuqa as soon as the man landed. "Do you know, I was about to choose that part myself!" he admitted.

"I thought as much," the Jajirat responded with a grin. "Why do you think I came here?"

"Pei-li!" Alp cried, recognizing his old companion. "I haven't seen you since Khitan days!"

"Well, I've seen *you*! When it became evident that the Khitans were not going to be it, I watched where you headed. I had to abort a going part to do it, but I got in there and snapped up the best prospect!"

"And Temujin didn't look like much!" Alp finished.

"Of course I didn't realize you were actually there. But when I saw how Temujin handled himself, I had a suspicion. So the first pretext I had to come and see for myself—"

"Right!" Alp said, holding no rancor. Pei-li had played it smarter and could not be faulted for that. "Wait till you meet Togrul!"

"I already have! That was another reason to come. We made a good team once—all the way up to Khagan! I think he has out-maneuvered the rest of us again—but we'll see."

"Yes," Alp agreed. "These Mongol politics are worse than the Uigur—and China is stronger now."

Togrul arrived. "But together we can do it!" he said. "It doesn't matter whom Jenghiz Qan derived from historically, so long as he manifests in the Game on schedule. I think the Machine will cover up if one of us pre-empts it. I figure it will happen in the next twenty Days."

"That makes us potential enemies . . ." Pei-li said.

"Stop thinking like a barbarian!" Uga snapped. "It makes us *rivals*—and we're friends."

"Still," Pei-li said thoughtfully, "a part that size—"

"Let the loser support the winner," Uga said. "And let the winner see that the loser has his chance to make a good score too. Jenghiz may be good for a million points—and his chief generals a hundred thousand each."

It made sense. Uga always did seem to have worked things out properly. Together they had three times the chance to become Jenghiz, and the support of the other two would sway other players toward the eventual winner. They could all do well and build this into an even better part than the Machine intended. "Agreed!" Alp said, and Pei-li nodded.

"Now let's see about recovering your wife," Uga said. "That *is* supposed to be the point of all this! I heard she's a pretty one."

Alp didn't answer. There was no sense in giving away exactly how important she was to him.

The three armies sufficed. They fell upon the Markit chief Toktagha in the Selenga River section of space and routed him. Temujin landed on the Markit campsite planet and ran among the tents even as the battle raged on land and in space. "Borte! Borte!" he cried.

201

A woman ran out heavily. "Temujin!"

It was Borte—and she was pregnant. Only a few hours had passed since she had been taken from him—but twelve Hours was equivalent to six months. The Machine had indulged in another expert job of makeup.

Was it Alp's child—or the brat of one of the Markit abductors? Alp had never had illusions about the use the Markit would have made of this lovely woman. But the possibility of pregnancy had not occurred to him before. It was only the Game—but if this had happened in history, it would have been vital to know the proper parentage. The agony of doubt was acute.

Borte waited anxiously for recognition, beautiful despite her condition, fearful that he would no longer want her.

Abruptly Alp realized that this question of paternity was beside the point. *He had her back!* All her future sons would be his, without doubt. There was only one solution to his dilemma: this first child would be his, no matter what. He would never make an issue of the matter.

Chapter 16

PROGRESS

Togrul went home, satisfied, but Jamuqa stayed on. Alp discovered that their present roles now gave him a greater community of interest with Pei-li, to whom he had not been that close as a Uigur. Uga had become too old, and he was not a Mongol. And—he had a disquieting amount of power.

For a Day-and-a-half Temujin and Jamuqa ranged the Mongol spaceways, enlisting the support of the other clans. Their defeat of the fierce Markit had won them authority, and the tribes were now rallying to the banners of these allies. The Mongols desperately needed a real leader. A Mongol hegemony was forming at last. Perhaps this time the old enemies would be vanquished: the traitorous Tatars, the Kin Chinese . . .

But there were differences between the allies, Alp and Pei-li. The demands of their new parts reversed their natural

203

temperaments; now Jamuqa was the adventurer, prone to innovations that were dramatic but not always sensible, while it was Temujin who took no unnecessary risks. "Take it easy!" he cautioned Pei-li repeatedly. "Remember how the great Uigur empire fell! We don't want to throw away Jenghiz Qan before either of us becomes Qan!"

"You're too damned conservative!" Pei-li said, smiling. "Nobody is going to conquer the world by plodding along safely!"

He was too far gone. He was a Galactic, carried away by the sensation of youth, overdoing it. The Game could not be won by a man who played it as a game!

Every so often Alp caught Pei-li eyeing Borte speculatively. This filled him with unspoken rage. She had delivered her son Jochi and now was pregnant again, but still . . . ! Temujin already had other wives, as befitted a Mongol leader; in many respects it was more economical to take an extra wife than to support a concubine. But the only one he cared about was Borte and the only sons he intended to recognize would be hers. Even the first . . .

Borchu the Arulat, Alp's first Mongol ally and general, was careful to keep his eyes on his own women. Was it that Pei-li recognized the maid of Uigur times?

It saddened Alp to see this wedge forming between them, for there were many qualities he respected in Pei-li, and they had worked well together as a Uigur team. But as the prospect for achieving the ultimate part grew, so did the competition between them. Power was tearing apart their friendship.

And Pei-li recognized this. "We're not good for each other, Alp," he said. "Not in this situation. When we both served Uga, it was easy to get along; now we are both striving to lead. We'd better separate and fight for it cleanly as Jamuqa and Temujin. That's the sporting way.''

Sport . . . But Alp had to agree. "Maybe we can get together again, some other part—or even some other Game.''

They shook hands, and Jamuqa took off, taking the fleets of his supporters with him. They amounted to about a third of the total Mongol force.

And what was Uga doing now, in his Kerayit kingdom? The only assembly that might have challenged his power had now broken in two.

For ten long Days Temujin and Jamuqa maneuvered, skirmishing with wandering fleets and lining up support for their separate causes, while the major cause of Jenghiz languished. The heirs of the old Mongol royalty preferred Temujin, seeing in him a more conservative, dependable, and perhaps docile leader—and he took care to foster that impression. But many dissidents supported Jamuqa, whose dramatic flair appealed to their frustrations. Horsemen rallied to Alp, herdsmen to Pei-li.

Alp drilled his Mongols constantly, forcing them to assemble their formations rapidly at a given signal. He had Qasar instruct them in accurate archery. The men, naturally unruly, did not like this—but Alp's new discipline was the strictest ever seen among Mongols. He was using Uigur techniques to forge a fighting machine to reckon with!

It was obvious that a unified Mongol Qanate was in the making, and this was something that every clan hungered for. It was past time to stop the internecine quarrels that weakened the Mongols and made them prey to the savage Markit to the west and Tatars to the east, with all the Steppe nomads intimidated and exploited by the Empire of Kin China to the south. As a Khitan, Alp had been betrayed by the Sung Chinese and the barbarian Jurchid nation who had taken over Khitan territory and formed the Kin Empire. As a Mongol, he was eager to be avenged on both Chinas—if he could only get around the determined competition of Jamuqa.

Alp realized that if many more Days went by without a decision, both he and Pei-li would lose out to some more enterprising chief . . . such as Uga. He doubted that the historical Jenghiz had had to cope with direct rivalry of this nature. But this was *not* history, it was Game—and stringent measures were required.

Temujin was now almost thirty years old, with four sons by Borte: Jochi, Jagatai, Ogodei and Tolui. The first was a promising lad of eleven (but was he really Temujin's own? Suppress that gnawing doubt!), the last a child of three. Jochi was coming up on the age Temujin had been when the Tatars poisoned his father. How young that seemed! It was past time to settle that account, too!

Alp had no intention of yielding his part the way Yesugei had! Let the Machine stop him if it chose! He was going to make his play for the big stakes!

Temujin called his followers together and had himself elected Qan of the Mongols, ignoring those under Jamuqa's banner. He chose the title Jenghiz: the Oceanic Qan. The date was 1196.

He waited apprehensively. Nothing happened. Apparently the Game Machine was not going to nullify Alp's presumption.

"Bastard!" Pei-li said in grudging private communication. "You had more nerve than I did. You took a leaf from Uga's book and simply declared yourself the winner! But we don't know how well that will work—and I haven't given up yet!"

And even Uga conveyed somewhat perfunctory congratulations. It had, after all, been his idea. Would he now be irked enough to make some serious countermove?

Alp knew he had not really won—yet. He now controlled half the true Mongols—who were the weakest of the major nations of the contemporary Steppe. In times past they had been more formidable. But the ravages of the Tatars and the Kin Empire had destroyed Mongol power a generation ago, and only now was it recovering.

But luck was with Alp. Soon after his declaration, a small formation of ships drifted in, long overdue for recharging. It was Uga himself, and his famished party.

"My brother conspired with the Naiman to dispossess me of my throne," Uga explained as he wolfed down the food Alp provided. "I fled to the southwest to ask help from the Empire of Black Cathay, but that turncoat threw me out! I wandered miserably around the Gobi desert section of space, seldom finding an adequate depot. Now I come to you. Remember how I helped you before—now I beg you to help me recover my throne!"

How the mighty had fallen! Alp saw he had no need to fear Uga's ambitions now. The man had bungled his part.

"Of course I'll help you!" Alp said graciously. "Think I want an unfriendly power on my southern flank?" But it was more than that, and they both knew it.

Alp provided the hard-pressed Kerayit chief with a fleet of ships, and in due course Togrul regained his throne. The favor had been returned.

The politics of the Game were fluid. The Tatars had taken to harassing the Kin Empire frontiers, and the Kin were becoming increasingly annoyed. King Ma-ta-ku the Jurchid, Lord of the Kin, had allowed the empire's military discipline to relax (folly! Alp muttered), so was not well equipped to deal with these Tatar raids. So he reversed his alliances and made a deal with Togrul of the Kerayit.

Alp assured Uga that he was still a loyal vassal despite the recent favor he had rendered, and willingly joined the mission against the Tatars. It wasn't as if the project were contrary to Mongol interest—and he wanted Kerayit support for his title of Qan.

In 1198 the massed fleets of Togrul and Temujin invaded the Tatar dominions from the northwest, while the Kin attacked from the southeast. The Tatar forces were decimated.

Yesugei had been avenged. The Game continued.

The Game-galaxy was seasonal. Day was summer and Night was winter, when the food depots closed down in the northern regions and in most of the mountains. With proper management a man could readily last out the Night, but this became more difficult with large formations. It was better for a full clan to move to winter pastures in the Galactic lowlands, where a limited number of depots remained in operation. This was general practice among the Mongols.

The Kiyat and their allies made this journey under Alp's

supervision. The migration would take half an Hour, for women, children and flocks moved slowly. The ships skirted the mountainous red giants, sticking to the star-free valleys between the great whorls of the Milky Way. There was a constant barrage of minor crises: drives breaking down, women having Game-babies, scouts mistaking the route. Alp loved it.

A scoutship flashed up to Alp's own. "Qan—an enemy approaches!"

Alp's pleasure vanished. "Who? How many ships?"

"Targ's Tayichiuts! Estimated thirty thousand."

Alp clapped his hand to his forehead. He had barely thirteen thousand ships in fighting trim here, since he had not anticipated the attack. Why hadn't his spies told him of Targ's plan?

Without specific orders, Alp's generals closed in about him: brother Qasar, not bright but still the fleet's finest bowshot; Borchu, masterful leader of men; young Subotai, brilliant tactician.

To fight or to run? In an instant Alp assessed the alternatives. If he fought, he would be surrounded by more than double his own number of fighting ships: Mongols who were as experienced as he in nomad combat. That was almost certain defeat. But if he fled, the slow supply ships that were the clan's cattle would be sacrificed, together with many of the women defending them. Borte was back in that pack, with her sons.

Alp did not need to appraise the terrain; he maintained familiarity with it as a continuing policy. The valley was narrow here, with only light-minutes separating the substantial gravity wells of the star ranges. Poor room for elaborate maneuvering, and a poor avenue for flight from enemy cavalry, as the valley would funnel the attacking horde right onto the Kiyat rear.

So he had to fight, however hopeless it seemed. But he could not make his stand across the width of the valley, for it was three dimensional. No matter how tight the east-west ranges were, and how firmly he braced for a north-south battle, the enemy could outflank him above and below. The rift extended for light years, that way.

They were passing a forest of minor debris: the dusty fragment of some bygone nebula, or perhaps a supernova. Horses could penetrate it, but only with extreme caution—a caution he could not now afford! But it served to block off one section of the northward thrust of the valley. A fighting fleet would have to circle the obstruction—and that could break up its formation and waste precious seconds. Quite suitable as a tactical barrier!

"Make a cube of the tent carts!" Alp ordered. "Man them with any women and boys who can handle a bow. Drive the supply wagons inside that enclosure. Put the whole thing directly south of the forest-nebula, five light-minutes."

Subotai's ship detached and went to execute the formation.

"Form the fighting ships into squadrons of a thousand each," Alp continued. "Ten cubed. Fill the space between the forest and the wagon-cube. Wait for their attack—and hold that formation!"

Borchu's face in the screen looked doubtful, but he did not protest. Odd indeed was this defense Alp had initiated—but in a hopeless case like this, conventional tactics would gain him nothing. Targ could consider any orthodox battle won!

The Kiyat had hardly set it up when the Tays fell upon them. The enemy squadrons were five hundred ships each: a cross section of a hundred, five ranks deep. There were sixty of them—compared to Alp's thirteen.

The front Tay squadrons halted in space, allowing more agile horsemen to pass through them. These were the archers, flashing out to loose their bolts in a shower before disappearing into the protection of the squadron mass. Such archery did not require specific aim; it depended on chance to bring down a percentage of the target force.

Conventional tactics—and Alp's forces were ready. His own archers, commanded by his brother Qasar, let fly with telling effect. Now all that bow-practice paid off; the men were not firing randomly but at selected spots. Tay losses appeared to be quadruple the Kiyat's.

But this was mere skirmishing. The Tays closed ranks and charged.

The warriors under Borchu met that rush with a dynamic countercharge. Because of the small compass of the engagement, restricted by the flanking nebula and wagon cube, only a portion of Targ's horde could engage Alp's at the moment. But his much greater overall strength was sure to tell in the end.

Something strange happened as the two forces met, their formations passing through each other while each horseman fired his arrows and hurled his spear at the enemy from a distance of a fraction of a light second. Actual sword fighting was not feasible in space, so the Game permitted the spears as an alternate mode despite the deviation from historical procedure. The Tay squadrons lost formation and drifted on, decimated—while the Kiyats went on to engage new squadrons.

Alp smiled as he watched his screens from his command post. Numbers *did* count—but in the immediate fray his squadrons of a thousand horses were twice as deep as the Tay squadrons of five hundred. That close-range superiority combined with the devastating accuracy of his archers gave him a tremendous spot advantage. Two of his ships engaged each of the enemy—when the Kiyats could have had a winning margin on a one-to-one basis. This broke the Tay formations and demoralized Targ's troops.

The Tay ships tried to retreat—and were cut down even more rapidly as they interfered with their own following formations. The momentum had swung to Alp's cavalry.

It was over in two Minutes—a full historical day—and the darkness of the Game-night descended. The instruments on all ships faded out, making accuracy of aim impossible.

Alp had won the day. Over five thousand Tay ships drifted in space, their stunned players waiting for the reclamation by the Game Machine. Seventy Tay subchiefs were made captive: they would join Alp's horde or be dispatched.

"But Targ!" Alp cried, distressed that his arch-enemy was not among them. "If Targ escapes, this victory is for nothing!"

One of his lieutenants signaled for attention. It was Chilaun the Suldu—the son of Chief Sorqan-Shira who had rescued Alp from Targ's cangue so many days ago and swore to have an accounting for the humiliation Targ had brought upon them then. Alp had not forgotten his own promise, and

Chilaun was the commander of one thousand horsemen. Alp granted him audience immediately.

"Targ did not escape," Chilaun said. Alp saw that the man was pale; he had suffered a glancing stun in battle.

"Who killed him?" Alp demanded, perversely annoyed that the privilege had not fallen to himself.

"I did," Chilaun said.

Alp's jealousy vanished. "Henceforth you are *tumen*—commander of ten thousand," he said. At the moment there were not that many men in the Mongol cavalry to command, and Borchu was already a *tumen*—but the honor was valid. With the power of Targ broken, Alp's dominion over the Mongol tribes would be extended. There would soon be troops to fill Chilaun's complement. Alp never forgot the men who served him in time of crisis, and he was glad Chilaun had proved himself.

Chapter 17

POWER

But success only brought more trouble. No sooner had Alp reorganized his forces after the Tay battle, than a conspiracy formed against him. It seemed that a number of clans and even nations were appalled at his victories, fearing that he was becoming too strong to stop. Their plot was nearly successful.

An unmarked ship visited the Mongol camp by night. It was Dai-Sechen the Qongirat, Borte's father. He insisted on transferring personally to Alp's horse in space.

"Father of my most cherished bride, you have no need to slink about like this!" Alp exclaimed. "I shall be happy to welcome you with ceremony in my *ger*, as befits your station and the esteem due you, and if you need anything at all—"

"If they learn of this, they'll kill me!" Dai-Sechen said. "I must speak and get out of here before dawn!"

"That's only a Minute away!" Alp said with a smile.

But the man was serious. "Temujin, they're plotting to murder you! My own clan is in on it. An ambush near Lake Buyur—"

Alp snapped to attention. "Stay with me, Chief! I'll put out word that your ship was brought down by raiders, so they won't know you reached me." He touched the communications stud. "Borchu! Chilaun! Here to me."

Dai-Sechen insisted on hurrying home again. Outwardly nothing changed. Temujin and Togrul proceeded on their scheduled trek to Buyur.

And slaughtered the ambushers. Thanks to Dai-Sechen, the Mongols and Kerayits had not been caught napping.

Then Jamuqa formed a counter-league, gathering in the remnants of the clans Alp had defeated, as well as elements of the Markit, Oirat, Naiman and Tatars. It was a formidable association, more powerful numerically than Alp's own. At a great assembly in 1201 Jamuqa had himself proclaimed Gur-Qan: the Emperor of Steppe.

Could he get away with that? The historical document had named Jenghiz Qan—but the Game did not follow history precisely. The name meant nothing if the power was not there.

There was nothing to do but meet this threat directly. If Alp dallied, Pei-li would come after him at his own convenience. It would all be very civilized on the personal level, and Alp privately admired the job Pei-li had done for his role of Jamuqa. But there was room for only one overall Qan of Steppe—and Alp had to be that one. Even if he hadn't been playing for the highest stakes—his own life in the real world—he would have responded to the political challenge raised here.

Alp laid his plans carefully. He cemented his pact with Uga, who now had assumed a title of his own: Wang Qan. "We're all competing for the ultimate Qan," Alp said to him, privately shuddering at this unhistorical duplication of the title. "If you and I do not act now, Jamuqa will walk away with it, and both of us will lose. Is that the way you want it?"

"I suppose you're right," Uga said reluctantly. "I don't like to fight against an old friend, but he *has* been pushing it recently. I really hadn't thought he would show that amount of skill on his own . . ."

That had surprised Alp, too. Almost as much as Uga's own ineptitude! Circumstance was bringing out new facets . . .

Together they amassed a great army and set out to meet the current enemy.

A supernova exploded before them.

"The Naiman magicians have raised this storm against us!" Alp exclaimed, frustrated.

Borchu laughed merrily. Alp, embarrassed, shut off his screen. He had forgotten, as he sometimes did: people no longer believed in magic, except when they called it God. *He* believed in it, of course, but it was not expedient to advertise that among the supposedly sophisticated Galactics.

But the storm was real enough. The fleet had to pick its way through the pelting stellar fragments—and Pei-lei's army was just beyond it. What a liability!

Still, the battle, when it came, was a great victory for Alp.

He did not catch Jamuqa, but he scattered the forces of the enemy.

Then his "enemy brethren," the Tays, made trouble again despite the loss of their chief Targ, and Alp had to campaign there. He thought it would be routine, but the Tays fought back with inspired ferocity and repulsed his forces. One arrow struck his ship glancingly; his horse was incapacitated and Alp himself was partially stunned. Helpless, he drifted out of control.

His captain Jelme spotted him and closed with his ship in space. Jelme, at great risk to himself, boarded, found Alp half-conscious, and carried him bodily to his own horse. They limped out of the fray.

"The battle!" Alp cried in more than physical anguish.

"The engagement is more than one attack," Jelme reassured him. "We shall regroup and take the Tay another time. Let Borchu command in your absence. Right now you have to rest; you took a bad stun."

Jelme had risked his own part to fetch Alp out of that mess. Yet Jelme was only one of many Mongol officers, and Alp knew that any of the others would have done the same. "How do I deserve such loyalty?" he asked as his body grew fevered from the pain of stun-recovery. "Real nomads would have let me die . . ."

"I don't know," Jelme said. "I suppose we are pretty far removed from the original Game plan—but we've got to play by the rules we know. You're the best leader we've had, so we have to stand by you. You seem to have a genuine feel for nomad tactics; you think of things the rest of us don't. Sometimes I wonder just what you do in civilian life."

Discreetly inquired—but Alp wasn't ready to tell others. Every man who learned his secret was a potential Pei-li, rival for the prize. "Nothing," he said with a wry grin.

Borte came to care for him, and soon he felt better.

A few Minutes later—the next day—Alp's forces smashed the Tay. Those surviving who would not swear loyalty to Temujin were systematically massacred; he had had too much of betrayal. The others were worked into the regular Mongol cavalry, spread about so as to lose their Tay connections. In the cartoon parlance, Kiyat had eaten Tay.

But there remained some fight in a few of the lesser Tay officers. The Tay had fought extremely well, and Alp wanted those officers—alive with him, or out of the Game. A group of six detached and fled. Alp recognized the markings of the lead ship. This was the warrior who had shot him down in battle!

Taking two hundred horse, Alp set out after the fugitive. The little band maneuvered cleverly but could not shake the experienced Kiyat pursuit. Twice Alp was sure he had them trapped—and twice he lost them again, shooting down only the lesser warriors while the leader escaped. Alp's fury was mixed with admiration: that was some Tay!

Then the enemy horse lost power. The lone fugitive slowed, and was surrounded by Alp's riders. "Who are you?" Alp demanded on the screen, close range.

The face of a youngster appeared. The man was no more than twenty, but there was a fire about him that was more than the foolhardiness of youth. "I am Jebe the Yesut."

"The Arrow," Alp mused, translating the name's literal

219

meaning. "A fitting designation." For there was no doubt of
Jebe's proficiency with the bow!

"You would never have caught me if my horse had been
fresh!" Jebe said defiantly.

"True," Alp agreed, amicable now that he had his man.
He wondered, as he did whenever he encountered a valiant
warrior, whether there could be original nomad blood in him.

"Give me a fair chance!" Jebe said, and it was a challenge, not a plea. "Let me have a fresh mount, and I'll fight
anyone you name. I want to die honorably."

Struck by his courage, Alp consented. It was understood
that Jebe would not be freed. If he overcame one Kiyat
warrior, he would have to meet another. But it was a fitting
demise for a brave man. If he took several with him, his
honor and his Game-score would be that much greater.

Alp designated a ship with a blaze of white on its nose,
and Jebe transferred. The Mongols made a sphere a light-
second across, and a volunteer champion entered to take up
Jebe's challenge. Contests of this nature were much enjoyed
by the players of Steppe, and the screens were alive with
private bets on the outcome.

Jebe accelerated toward the Kiyat, but did not fire. He
galloped on through the center, gaining speed, and in a
quarter-second was up against the containing wall. One of his
accurate arrows brought down the ship nearest him; then he
struck another with his spear and broke through the hole.

The Kiyats swarmed after him—but Jebe had a full second's start and a fresh horse. They could not catch him. Alp
swore violently in Uigur, furious at having been so readily

tricked by a mere Galactic. But in a moment his expletives turned to laughter. That Jebe possessed true nomad cunning!

A few Minutes later the white-nosed horse returned. A thousand Mongol ships went out to bring it down—but Alp made them hold their fire. "What mischief are you up to now, Arrow?" he demanded, suppressing a smile.

"I have only hinted at what I can do," Jebe said insolently. "Now I'd like to do it for you, because you gave me my fair chance and you are the most worthy Qan in the Game."

For a moment Alp hesitated, uncertain whether to blot out this impudence or accept the services of a remarkable player. Jebe might be a Tay agent yet . . . no, after Alp was through with the Tay clan, there would not be anything there for an agent to serve! Better to trust this man's proffered loyalty, as he had done with others.

"All right, Jebe," he said. "I'll give you command of ten horsemen. Show me what you can do *for* me, and you will prosper."

Then Alp proceeded to reduce the Tatars as he had the Tays, massacring the warriors and incorporating their women and children into his own tribe. Jebe did well and was promoted; but Subotai did even better, tricking the Tatars into a poor defensive posture at the outset of that campaign.

Yet another coalition formed against him, led again by Jamuqa. Alp had to campaign continuously against the Markit, Naiman, and fragments of other tribes. More Minutes passed in battle, and though Alp won steadily, he seemed no closer to achieving the nomad unity he sought. But the worst was yet to come.

*　　*　　*

By 1203 Alp's relations with Togrul the Kerayit—his old friend Uga—had deteriorated. Togrul had undertaken several missions on his own, without advising his ally Temujin, and had failed to split the Game-spoils with him. Once, during a joint engagement against the Naiman, Togrul had decamped in the night, leaving Temujin to extricate himself alone, with great difficulty. Uga later apologized, claiming it was an error, that his runners had been ambushed before reaching Alp with news of his plans. But the circumstance was suspicious, and Alp was forced to wonder just how far the judgment of his old friend could now be trusted. Uga was making too many mistakes.

Still, it was welcome news when a messenger arrived from Togrul with an invitation to a reconciliation feast. Together they could put down Jamuqa once and for all. "I shall attend at once," Alp announced.

But no sooner had the Kerayit horseman departed than Alp's screen lighted again. It was old Munlik, his adviser since childhood. While Alp had been carving a Steppe empire Munlik had quietly allied himself most cosily by marrying Temujin's mother Oelun-eke. Alp disliked him no less for that but had to make the best of it. The widow did need a husband. Munlik's seven grown sons had become increasingly obstreperous, now considering themselves to be the equals of Temujin's own brothers: did they not have the same mother? Old Munlik himself was a crafty one—but loyal, now that Alp was Qan.

"What is it, my father?" Alp inquired politely, suppressing the quirk of annoyance he felt at having to use this address.

"Son, listen to me," Munlik said greasily. "I served your father when he was invited to a feast. Had he but listened to me then . . ."

An ugly shock ran through Alp. There was no doubt about what the old man meant—but Alp had heard similar suspicions before. "Are you implying that my honorable ally Wang Qan would betray me?" he demanded tersely.

"Son, I know you don't like me—but when have I ever misinformed you?" Unctuous but accurate! "Togrul's son is close to Jamuqa, and he has prevailed on his father to join Jamuqa against you. They have set an ambush to kill you. My spies know this."

Was the old man trying to force a wedge between Alp and Uga? Maybe—but he would hardly dare if there were not some element of truth to it, for Munlik knew Alp would check. Munlik had an excellent spy system, and a success of this nature would substantially enhance the house of Munlik in the Mongol hierarchy and assure his sons of increasing power. And Alp knew what Munlik could not: that Uga and Pei-li were old friends who would find collaboration easy. Uga's claim to the leading role had been weakened to the point of uselessness; if he had finally given it up, he might be promoting it for his friend. What quicker way than treachery?

"Show me your evidence," Alp said, curtly.

Munlik did. It was convincing. Alp had to make a pretext to cancel the rendezvous with Togrul, carefully concealing his knowledge of the plot. He was furious and heartsick. His friendship with Uga—and with Pei-li too—pre-dated every other Game acquaintance, and he had relied on that continuing liaison more than he had realized. But there was no doubt Uga had turned against him—secretly.

There was nothing to do but prepare for war. Togrul was now an enemy, the worst kind, and had to be eliminated from the Game.

Alp's preparations could not be concealed entirely. Togrul, realizing that his gambit stood exposed, massed an army of his own and moved into Mongol space, hoping to surprise Alp.

The battle was terrific. Never before had Alp fought directly against the Kerayit, and he discovered them to be formidable warriors. The Wang Qan's fleet outnumbered Alp's, and this time no tricks of deployment sufficed to reverse the odds. The Mongol officers wrought seeming miracles of infiltration, planting the banner of the nine yaktails on a planet behind the enemy formation, and they managed to cripple the horse of Togrul's scheming son. But Borchu was wounded, and so was Temujin's own son Ogodai. Slowly, relentlessly, the Kerayit pressed their advantage.

Alp had to retreat before that disciplined array. He retained the nucleus of his cavalry, but it was now in no condition to match the Kerayit. Togrul's troops followed, and it was all Alp could do to keep out of their clutches. Never before had a numerically inferior force put up such strong resistance to the mighty Kerayit—but this was little consolation to Alp. He had miscalculated, and Uga had won the day.

It might have been a different matter, had Alp had more time to prepare. But the Steppe cared little for excuses. Alp had been deceived by his reliance on a friendship carrying over from another part—and had paid heavily for that foolishness. Now the scales were off his eyes—too late.

He came to the region of space frequented by the Qongirat, his wife's clan. Dai-Sechen was sympathetic to Temujin, but his tribe belonged to the enemy alliance. There was little he could do openly. It was a difficult situation.

Borte was still lovely after eighteen Days of marriage, and still Alp's favorite wife—in fact, still the only one he really cared about. He did his duty by his other wives, but didn't even keep track of their sons. Now Borte went among her people, pleading as only a woman could the cause of kinship. She reminded them how well the Qan had treated her, and how he had even gone to war to rescue her from the Markit, and how he honored all her sons without distinction between them, even the first . . .

It was effective. This was a type of loyalty the Qongirat understood. They joined Temujin and gave his party the help it needed. What a woman he had married!

Still he had to retreat to the cold marches that constituted the northern rim of the galaxy. Winter was longer here and the depots farther apart; few journeyed here from preference. Many of Alp's followers deserted him, making his case even worse.

And he had aspired to be Qan of all Steppe!

He sent a reproachful message to Togrul, reminding him of past services, such as the time he had helped the man recover his Kerayit throne. "Weakened by hunger, you came on like a dying fire. I gave you food, ships, supplies. You were thin; within an Hour I had fattened you again." He did not specifically mention their illicit project to anticipate the thrust of the Game, but he knew Uga would remember. To betray that friendship for the greed of a higher Game score, when he *knew* what a loss would mean to Alp's Galactic survival . . .

Was this the reason the Machine had not interfered with their manipulations? There was something about that that he could never quite remember . . . Had the Machine known that success would split them apart and cost them everything? It was certainly hard to get ahead!

Yet Alp condemned himself, too, for not anticipating this. The Game was nearing its conclusion, surely. Now that they all had Mongol parts in the period of the historical Jenghiz, Uga and Pei-li did not need Alp any more. They were Galactics, not nomads; they did not share his philosophies. He should have known they were demons at heart, not to be trusted.

He could foresee the logical future. The various conspirators would eliminate each other, and the real Qa-Qan, the "Greatest Ruler," would emerge from the ruin just as history had planned. The Machine had it arranged, after all . . .

Alp moped only a few Minutes. He had been in tight spots before, in this part and in others and in life itself, and was not going to give it up now. The godlike Machine seemed never to interfere overtly; it followed the rules of the Game in order to mold its history. If Alp overcame all obstacles and managed after all to occupy the spot Jenghiz Qan was scheduled for, the Machine would have to go along with him, rather than distort a much larger section of history by removing him.

Or so he had to assume. Most Galactics believed it was

226

impossible for a player to beat the Game plan—but Alp was not Galactic. That was the trouble!

Alp spent the summer of 1203 at the very fringe of the galaxy, staring out at the emptiness of intergalactic space. Did they have other Games going on in other galaxies? What *were* other galaxies? His Galactic knowledge had faded, as Uga once had warned, and he remembered very little outside the Game. Borte would help him in the demon world, if he ever reached it, but still—still it made him profoundly uneasy. Perhaps death was the simplest way out . . .

This was space madness! He had heard of it now and then in the course of the Game, but not before comprehended it. The universe was large . . . a wondering whether anything at all had meaning . . .

For six Hours he endured it; then he had to return to the more familiar, comfortable stamping grounds, no matter what awaited him there. Deep space was not for nomad minds!

The enemy plotters had fallen out among themselves during his absence. Jamuqa had conspired to assassinate the Wang Qan—but Togrul had discovered it in time and driven out his former friend. So Jamuqa the Gur-Qan had taken refuge with the Naiman. One of his associates actually joined Temujin.

Yes, Alp's position had improved materially during his summer's exile, thanks to the dishonor among thieves.

Uga had made a fatal mistake when he practiced to betray Alp. For Alp was a true Steppe nomad, born a Uigur, among whom betrayal was punishable by dismemberment and death. He had kept faith with his friend—but now that Uga had broken faith, he was an enemy. There was no such thing as keeping faith with an enemy. A whole new set of standards prevailed.

When it came to loyalty, the Uigur was absolute. And when it came to deceit, he was a master.

Alp's new campaign had begun with his message of reproach. He continued with a barrage of false pleas for rapprochement with the Wang Qan, Togrul. Temujin's brother Qasar made contact, for Qasar's family had fallen into the power of the Kerayit. Qasar really believed in the mission, so Uga's trick truth-swords could not give him away. And Uga, thus misjudging the temper of his adversary, was lulled. He actually thought all was forgiven.

Alp made a secret march through space. He also disguised himself and went into the enemy lines to complain of illtreatment—and to admit incidentally that Temujin's horde was still far away. The Kerayit officers, not to be fooled, sent him back with an escort of several ships to check for themselves. Togrul might be foolish; his strategists weren't.

Naturally the party encountered the deploying Mongol forces. But Alp, alert to what to look for, was first to spy the advancing fleet. He knew that the Kerayit, well mounted, could turn and escape, giving the alarm—if they realized. Quickly he reined in his horse.

"What are you doing, deserter?" his suspicious escort-captain demanded. "We have a long way yet to ride—if what you say is true."

"A malfunction in my engine," Alp said. It was good to lie freely again! "I think I can fix it in a moment."

"We'll give you a remount."

"No need! This has happened before, but I like this horse. Just let me nudge the panel, here . . ."

And while he stalled, to the sputtering frustration of the captain, the Mongol vanguard surrounded the Kerayit party. There was not even a fight; the Kerayit were taken prisoner, and the secret was preserved.

"You should not take such risks, Qan!" Jebe reproved him on the screen, smiling because it was exactly the type of exploit Jebe himself indulged in.

"*Qan?*" the Kerayit captain demanded, astounded. Had he but known . . .

Not long thereafter the Mongols fell upon the Kerayits, who were taken utterly by surprise and scattered. Wang Qan did not retain a loyal cadre this time, and there was no ally Temujin to succor him. He fled to Naiman space where, unrecognized, he was shot down. That quickly did his elimination from the Game follow his defeat.

Alp sighed, his rancor gone. He had done what was necessary. But he wished it had not *been* necessary. If only Uga had kept faith!

The surviving Kerayit made submission to Temujin. Alp resettled their elements among the various Mongol clans, his standard precaution. Never again did he intend to face a unified enemy Kerayit nation! In time the Kerayits would be absorbed, and they would be Mongols, with complete loyalty to the Mongol Qan. Uga had hoped to assume the Mongol title; Alp had converted the Kerayits to Mongols in another way!

Now only one major independent power remained in central Steppe: the Naiman. They controlled the western part,

229

while Alp controlled the east. Jamuqa was with the Naiman now, though he no longer had the nerve to sport the pretentious Gur-Qan title. Alp knew that he could not rest until that threat had been eliminated.

Alp reorganized and drilled the enlarged Mongol forces, forging them into the most formidable fleet yet. Then in 1204 he prepared to move against the Naiman.

Jamuqa, awed by the force Alp had mustered, fled with his Jajirat clansmen just before the battle was joined. Alp, advised of the desertion, sneered; without Uga, Pei-li turned out to be nothing more than an opportunistic coward!

Meanwhile, the bulk of the Naiman stood firm. Qasar commanded the Mongol center and showed consummate leadership: courage counted for more than craft, this time. The Naiman were pushed back, decimated. Their Tayang was wounded. Barely clinging to Game-life, he was conveyed to a small planet to the rear of his lines. Alp had a spy in that entourage who managed to broadcast what followed:

TAYANG: "Who are these who pursue our ships with such devastation?"

FIRST OFFICER: "They are the hunting dogs of Temujin: Jebe the Arrow, Jelme the Devout, Subotai, Borchu, Qasar . . . They feed on spaceships and are leashed with lasers; their skulls are of brass, their teeth hewn from primeval rock; their tongues are swords and their hearts of iron!"

SECOND OFFICER: "What should we do, Tayang?" (Silence.)

THIRD OFFICER: "Arise, Chief! Your wives and mother await you!"

(No response.)

Then the last of the Naiman returned to their ships and resumed the hopeless battle. Alp, moved by their courage in adversity, would have spared them. But they fought on resolutely until the last man was eliminated from the Game.

"They must have had a great leader!" Alp said, shaking his head. Would his own troops serve him like that, after he died?

The bulk of the Naiman populace now submitted to Alp. But Jamuqa remained to be hunted down. That was to take two more Days but was inevitable, for Alp had conquered Steppe.

Chapter 18

QAN

For the moment there were the Naiman to be assimilated into the empire. First Alp checked the officers and aristocracy among the captives, determining their potential usefulness to the new order. It was his policy to waste nothing, and he considered human skills to be the greatest resource of all. By properly utilizing the talents of the men in his empire, he could forge it into a stronger power than had ever been seen in Steppe before. One that could successfully tackle the perennial enemy of all the nomads: China.

Some of the captives were well-dressed Uigurs. Alp recognized them instantly, for they were his kind, even when only players in the Game. He had paid scant attention to the political affairs of the diminished Kingdom of the Uigur, fearing that this could adversely effect his objectivity and make him prone to mistakes. He was a Mongol now and had

233

to cultivate Mongol thinking, lest he slip and lose everything
. . . as he almost had. But he was aware that the Uigurs,
after being displaced by the Kirghiz in 840, had settled in the
Tarim Basin of the galaxy and become civilized farmers and
traders. Later barbarian powers had drawn on Uigur literacy
and been somewhat civilized by it—such as the Khitans and
more recently the Naiman. So the presence of a number of
Uigurs here was not surprising. Now Alp had reason to
cultivate them specifically, for the Kingdom of the Uigur was
his new neighbor to the southwest. He was in a fashion
returning to his homeland!

Alp's hands were sweaty, but his voice was steady. "Who
are those?" he inquired, as if he did not know.

"They are savants, astrologers, physicians, scribes," came
the answer. "They read the stars, make predictions, care for
sick women, write letters."

"That one," Alp said, pointing to a minister holding a
curiously wrought gold object.

"I am Tata-tunga, keeper of the Tayang's seal," the Uigur
said.

Alp froze. Tata-tunga in person! The author of the historical manuscript that had led to the entire Mongol quest! What
did this portend?

But he kept his voice even. "The Naiman's power is
broken. You are a Uigur; you owe the Tayang nothing more."

But the Uigur would not speak against the dead Tayang.
"He was a good master."

Alp liked this. The man who was loyal to one leader even
after death would be loyal to another—once won over. "What
is the purpose of this object?"

Tata-tunga lifted the gold. "This is the Tayang's seal. Whenever he made an order he stamped it with this seal to prove the order was not forged. No other seal duplicates this pattern."

This was something new to Alp. He had been aware of seals but had thought they were relics of the ancient western peoples like the Sumerians. So now the nomads were finding use for them! "Who writes out the orders?"

"I do, usually," Tata-tunga said.

Naturally the man was literate! But not the way Alp was, this player would write in Galactic script, not Uigur. "You will join my court," Alp said, "granting me the same loyalty you gave your former master. You will arrange to have a seal made for me—not gold, something more precious. Jade, I think. And you will instruct my children in writing and in history." He thought a moment, then added: "And you will compile a survey of national mythologies—Mongol, Naiman, Uigur—and Khitan. The process of empire is unkind to separate subcultures, so we want an accurate record."

Tata-tunga looked at him with new appraisal, then acknowledged with a formal tilting of his head. An extremely able scholar had just been added to the empire. And so long as this Uigur remained in Alp's service, Temujin had to be Jenghiz.

Meanwhile, Alp's enormously increased power brought new problems. He was not accustomed to the niceties of organizing a real empire, and leaned heavily on the intelligent Tata-tunga from the outset of their acquaintance. The man knew more about government than Alp did. If Tata-tunga were a true representation of the Uigur original—and Alp's secret document suggested this was the case—the breakup of the Uigur empire was as much blessing as tragedy. Uigurs now ran a larger portion of Steppe than they could have on their own. Stripped of their military role, they had concentrated on education—a more enduring asset.

Alp had his first serious taste of palace intrigue. Old Munlik, Temujin's stepfather, remained a capable adviser. There was so much work to be done that Alp could not conveniently dispense with his services, apart from the potential stickiness of eliminating a technical relative. So Alp continued to tolerate him, and Munlik continued to handle the myriad noisome details of nomad organization and discipline with unquestionable loyalty to Alp's interest . . . and that was one of the things Alp disliked about the man. The darker side of Alp's personality was mirrored in Munlik too clearly . . .

But Munlik's seven sons lacked their father's discretion. One among them, Tab-tangri, was a shaman: a worker of magic. Few Galactics actually believed in sorcery, but it was considered valid in the context of the Game, and Tab did have an impressive array of tricks. He could make a burning fire appear in his hand, then quench it and show his hand ungloved and unburned. He could make his ship vanish from the screens of other ships as if he had fallen into another continuum. And he had helped Alp by proclaiming that Temujin was the man chosen by the Game Machine to be the next and only lord of all Steppe, the Great Qan. Many dubious allies were swayed by this, and it enhanced the image Alp was so laboriously forming among the various Steppe peoples: his inevitable supremacy.

But Tab was personally ambitious and vied with Temujin's own sons for influence at the Mongol court. He became insolent, and worked insidious mischief. He quarreled with Temujin's brother Qasar, and when unable to move the stout warrior, set upon Qasar's ship with several of his brothers, crippling it.

Qasar survived and promptly complained to Alp. "That bastard Tab tried to eliminate me!" he shouted, redfaced on the screen.

At first Alp didn't believe it. "You—a leader of the Mongol archers? How could he touch you?"

Black rage showed on Qasar's face, and he cut the connection. Alp hadn't meant to insult him—but certainly Qasar should never have been taken unawares by the likes of Tab! It was a good lesson.

Next Tab himself called. "The Spirit has revealed to me a command from Eternal Heaven," he intoned in that shamanistic way of his. "Temujin will reign first, and after him Qasar. How fortunate to have such a brother!" He faded.

This hardly seemed like a quarrel with Qasar! Tab was endorsing him for Qan, just as he had endorsed Temujin before. Why was Qasar so surly?

But as Alp thought about it, he liked it less. Why should Qasar rule after him? Was something going to happen to Temujin?

He imagined Qasar pre-empting the empire, dispossessing Temujin as Togrul's brother had dispossessed the Kerayit Qan. Such things happened to the unwary.

A fury built up in Alp. He was not going to be ousted like that! He called his personal guard: "Arrest Qasar!"

Qasar was bound and brought to the Qan's pavilion on the planet of Karakorum. Alp drew his sword, shaking with fury. "Do you dare to plot against your own brother?" he demanded.

Qasar looked confused. This ploy only inflamed Alp's nomad rage. "I'll kill you right now!" he roared.

Qasar looked at him as if he were insane. But as Alp lifted the sword to smite that expression away, their mother Oelun-eke rushed in. She went to Qasar and released his bonds while Alp stood somewhat stupidly, sword in hand. Of all times!

Oelun-eke turned to Temujin and removed her dress, baring her breasts. "These breasts suckled you both!" she cried. "How can you quarrel between yourselves? Hasn't Qasar always served you loyally? When did he ever have ambition for more?"

Alp's rage turned to embarrassment. Even though it was all a drama in the Game, he hated being exposed to this sort of scene. He might question the loyalty of almost anyone, but never that of his mother. "I am ashamed," he said, leaving the pavilion.

Afterwards he wondered just what had happened to him. Of *course* Qasar wouldn't plot against him! The man was too stupid to be other than loyal. *Tab* was the schemer. He had so cleverly planted his poison barb without actually accusing Qasar of anything . . .

Alp had almost made a bad mistake. He was over-extended, making snap judgments, turning against his most loyal allies. As Uga had, before the end . . . He needed to ease up before he let schemers like Tab worm him into real trouble.

But Tab was not finished. He gathered quite a following among the Mongol horde. Galactic players were more credulous than they pretended; many of them were coming to believe the shaman's magic was genuine. Alp, who had experience with real magic in life, could tell the difference, fortunately.

Soon Tab turned against Temujin's youngest brother, Temuge, catching him on the streets of the city and forcing him to kneel to the sons of Munlik. Temuge was a real firebrand, and this was a terrible humiliation for the brother of the Qan!

Unlike Qasar, Temuge did not complain. Perhaps he was afraid it would only lead to another scene with the Qan! But the story was circulated, and this time it was Alp's beloved wife Borte who interceded. "If even during your lifetime your brothers are open to insult," she said, "what will happen to your sons after your death?"

Her pointed words affected Alp as the words of his brothers had not. His sons were threatened! Tab had overstepped his bounds, and had to be dealt with.

But the Qan was supposed to be an objective arbiter—and Mongols were forbidden to settle personal quarrels by arms. Alp had laid down that doctrine himself, enforcing it by the death penalty; he could not be the one to violate it. Also, Tab was a powerful political force in his own right, and his untimely removal could trigger a disastrous split in the Mongol ranks that would cost Alp his base of power.

This was one problem that Munlik could not solve, for

Munlik's own sons were the cause of the mischief. And Tata-tunga wisely disdained to participate in palace intrigue, however clever he was in organizing the larger empire. Alp had to work this out by himself.

Well, how would clever Jamuqa have done it, or shrewd Togrul? Or Munlik himself, had this involved some other man's son? How did a ruler dispose of a ranking figure in his court, while maintaining the facade of neutrality? This was unclean business, but Alp saw what had to be done.

He called Munlik on the screen. "You and your sons will visit my *ger* for conference," Alp said.

"Delighted!" Munlik agreed, anticipating further enhancement of his influence.

Then Alp called Temuge: "Munlik and his sons are visiting me for conference. Come also, if you choose." He paused, noting his brother's perplexity. "It does not behoove the Qan to take sides. Deal with someone as pleases you."

Now Temuge's eyes lighted. Alp had let his brother know he would not interfere, keeping his hands technically clean. Temuge knew that Alp knew of his fury with Tab . . .

In a few Minutes Munlik and his sons arrived. They seated themselves, weapons left outside the *ger*, according to protocol. Then Temuge appeared, unarmed but fierce. "Let's see how you do on your own!" he cried, seizing Tab by the throat.

Munlik and the others stood in alarm and sought to interfere. "Go outside and settle your difference!" Alp cried with unfeigned annoyance. He had expected more subtlety than this!

Tab was a larger man than Temuge and a skilled brawler.

240

He was quite ready to fight, especially since he obviously had the right of it and the Qan had given permission. Angrily the two went out, while Alp gestured Munlik and the others to resume the conference.

There was a scream, then silence.

Now Alp and the others looked out. Temuge stood there, untouched. Tab lay on the ground, obviously out of the Game. Three guards stood near the tent. It took no great perception to know that there had been an ambush.

Munlik, white-faced, turned to Alp. "O Qan, I have served you until this day . . . ."

Alp was alone in the tent. The six strong sons made as if to set upon him physically. He had no weapon.

"Aside!" he said peremptorily, brushing by them. They might have laid hands on him despite their awe of his office and the certain consequence of such action; but Temuge and the three guards now stood at the entrance, seeming rather eager for a pretext for mayhem, and Qasar was coming down the street by seeming coincidence with another troop of warriors. In fact, there were suddenly a great many loyal and strong Mongols in the vicinity.

The sons of Munlik gave way. ". . . and I shall continue to serve you," Munlik finished bravely.

Then Alp told him: "You did not teach your sons proper obedience. Tab conspired against my interests, so I removed my protection from him. See that it doesn't happen again; I have no other quarrel with you and need your continuing service as a loyal adviser."

Munlik nodded gravely. He had been outmaneuvered, his

own tactics used against him; but he was being allowed to save face.

So it ended—a difficult situation, but a useful lesson to those who thought they could manipulate the Qan. Even Qasar's understandable grudge abated, now.

In 1206 Alp called a great assembly of all the Mongols and their subject tribes of the Steppe and had himself once more proclaimed Jenghiz Qan—leader of all the nomads. This time it was real.

Chapter 19

RECKONING

Mongol was now a highly disciplined giant, and there was little danger of his falling apart into dwarves again. He fought well, riding up on his stocky, fiery horse when the enemy least expected it, but avoiding battle when the enemy was ready to fight. Sometimes Mongol would feign retreat, as though afraid—and when the other giant tried to chase him, Mongol would lure him into some trap, then shoot an arrow into him from behind. When the other was confused and hurt by the arrow in his posterior, Mongol would charge in screaming and cut him to pieces with his sword.

Now that Mongol was strong, he set about the usual business of the giants of Steppe: conquering China. Just for practice he started with Hsi-Hsia, the dwarf in Tibet, who was the weakest of the three Chinese powers. Hsi-Hsia's territory controlled the old Silk Road, and Mongol hankered

243

for more silk underwear, so this was as good a place to begin as any.

But Mongol, for all his skill in open-country battle, was not much good at attacking a castle. He tore up Hsi-Hsia on the field, but when the dwarf hid behind his walls Mongol couldn't get at him. He tried and tried, riding around the castle and shooting arrows at it, but with little success.

Mongol raided Hsi-Hsia's territory several times, then tried to get into the castle by moving the Yellow River away. But he wasn't a very good dam builder either, so that didn't work. Still, he made things so rough for Hsi that the dwarf agreed to be his vassal after all.

Now Mongol turned against Kin, the Tungus giant of north China—the one who had ousted civilized Khitan. As it happened, Kin was growing a new head. This new head told Mongol to get down on his knees before it. Mongol's own head, Jenghiz Qan, flew into a rage. "I won't humble myself before this imbecile!" he cried, spitting at Kin.

Mongol made deals with a couple of dwarves in Kin's territory: Ongut, of the Turk family, who guarded the frontier; and Khitan himself, who now lived on the other side. Naturally Khitan didn't have much affection for Kin! So while Ongut let Mongol in on the northwest, Khitan helped him on the northeast.

In 1211 Mongol began his war with Kin. It actually took him more than twenty Days to finish it, because he still didn't know how to capture a castle. So he would storm in and tear things up and take booty, then go back home. That gave Kin a chance to catch his breath. Also, Mongol was used to getting rid of enemies by chopping them up or eating them whole—but the giants of China were so fat that he couldn't possibly chop up everything or eat it without turning Chinese himself—a fate worse than death! And Kin himself had been a barbarian only a hundred Days ago, so he fought back pretty hard. On top of all that, Mongol was already getting into fights with other dwarves, so he wasn't paying proper attention to Kin. This made it a long campaign.

Actually, Kin had several castles in his large territory, and Mongol did finally capture one, in 1215. He had never been in a castle before, and he just didn't understand it, so he tore it up and then set it on fire. It was really too bad to waste it like that; but the barbarian was merely destroying what he didn't understand.

Mongol turned this battle over to one of his hands, while his head Jenghiz concentrated on the next war. This was with the large dwarf, Black Khitan, derived from a fragment of the old Khitan giant that fled Kin further to the west. But Black Khitan was sick, having lost his old head and grown a new one that he didn't like, and he really was glad to join Mongol and be done with it.

Next west was the small giant Khwarizm, who was another matter. He was new, having only acquired his territory a few Days before, and he had a hot temper. Mongol wanted to trade, since the other end of the Silk Road was in Khwarizm's territory; but the little giant pinched Mongol's fingers and insulted him. So the next Day Mongol rode against him, fully armed.

Khwarizm's fighting strength in that region was greater than Mongol's for he was in his home territory while Mongol had to climb over the mountain between them to get there.

Furthermore, a large part of Mongol was still fighting tough Kin in the east. But Mongol was a tremendous giant now, and extremely well disciplined, and in just a couple of Days he demolished Khwarizm. He was well on the way to mastering the entire world.

In 1227 Mongol lost his head, that had served him so well for over twenty Days.

And Alp was out of the Game. The action continued, both in the galaxy and in cartoon summary, but his role was done. Alp had somewhat over one million points and was the high scorer of the Game to date. It was time to retire; he would never have a better opportunity to obtain Galactic status.

His Audience Quotient had fared well too: average steady viewing had risen to a phenomenal seven million. Alp no longer cared how many thousands of spectators had watched his every act, whether in battle or with his wives; the important thing was his tremendous success with the part.

"But I am curious about one thing," he said to the Game Machine, who always seemed to have the time for an individual conversation despite its colossal responsibilities elsewhere. "When I sought the documents, you did not interfere because no one complained. But in matters of historical accuracy you do exert control. Why did you permit me to steal the role of Jenghiz Qan?"

"There was no theft," it replied equably. "Temujin was the historical Jenghiz Qan—or Genghis Khan, as it is rendered in some texts."

"But I stretched my part way beyond history! Collusion

with Togrul and Jamuqa, and their own assumptions of Qan Titles—''

''No, you followed the script with admirable accuracy, all of you. Jamuqa was indeed Gur-Khan for a time, and Togrul used his Chinese title Wang Khan for years until his death. Jenghiz Qan is a very difficult part to play properly, so the Machine saw to it that a specially qualified man was available. In past renderings of the Game of Steppe there have been distortions because of the inadequacy of Galactic players; people who shied away from the necessities of barbarian power or were unable to scheme in the fashion of the true nomad.''

Alp perceived that he owed more to this intelligent Machine than he had thought. His very presence here in the galaxy must have been arranged by it . . . ''Nomad no more,'' he said. ''Now I need to buy my citizenship in the galaxy.''

''Why should you wish to do this?''

''You know why, Machine! How do I go about it?''

''There is no need.''

''You know there *is* a need. Death may mean nothing to you, since you're not alive; but if I set foot outside the Game—''

''You have been pardoned your origin,'' it said.

''. . . the police will send me back to—*what?*''

''There was considerable sentiment encouraging your pardon, once the facts were known. You are now a prominent figure in the galaxy, Alp the Uigur. The Galactic Counsel passed a special resolution by unanimous acclaim. Keep your winnings; you are now a rather wealthy Galactic Citizen.''

247

Alp was amazed. "How did they know—?"

"The Game Machine, by permitting your abduction into this framework, assumed a certain responsibility for your welfare. That was the essence of its testimony before the Galactic Council. It must be understood that the purpose of the Machine was not philanthropic; it was merely promoting a more effective, entertaining and educational Game by introducing a genuinely historical figure and providing him with strong motivation to succeed. You were never actually in danger of extradition—"

But Alp was no longer paying attention. A panel had opened, and there stood Koka/Borte, the Galactic girl with strong nomad ancestry. No doubt the Machine had arranged that too, but Alp didn't care. She was not nine as he had met her, or in her fifties as he had left her. She was her real age, which seemed to be about his own, and she was absolutely lovely.

She smiled at him expectantly. Now he could marry her all over again, dispensing with the need to maintain secondary wives. She would take thousands of days to grow old! No Game part could match that luxury!

"And don't broadcast this, Machine!" he said as she came into his grasp.

Author's Note for TOR edition of Steppe

By this time you probably realize that the history related in *Steppe* is genuine, whether presented in Game-form or cartoon-form. You have just had a fairly comprehensive course in Central Asian history. History fascinates me, but evidently it doesn't interest publishers, so I had to mask it as space opera. Unfortunately I didn't mask it well enough, and publishers realized that there was educational value here, and shied away. I feel that this is a good way to make history interesting to those who normally find it boring, so I really enjoyed the challenge of this project. I generally do have more than one level to my writing, for those who care to fathom it. But relevance and serious content can be hazardous to a fiction-writer's career.

1972 was a good year for writing, but a poor year for sales. I completed five novels—*Hard Sell, A Piece of Cake*

249

(Triple Detente), Kiai!, Steppe, and *Ghost*—and sold one, *Rings of Ice,* which I hadn't yet written. That one was my first sale based on a summary; after that I usually did not write novels until they sold, and as a result my rejects diminished and my income tripled. So this was a significant turning point; every novel I have completed from that time on has been sold. But of the five for 1972, only three have been eventually published, and one of those—*Steppe*—only in Europe. And thereby hangs a tale.

You see, they didn't want *Steppe* in Europe, either. But a British hardcover publisher was interested in getting into the SF genre, and so was picking up what it could get from the major names—and some lesser ones, such as Anthony. So it solicited and bought an available Anthony novel in 1975. This was *Rings of Ice,* published in America the year before. That's right: the novel I sold from summary, after sustaining six successive washouts. (Six? Yes—there was also *Mer-Cycle,* completed late in 1971.)

Fine for the publisher. But one novel does not a program make. So they (I have never been able to decide whether a publisher is singular or plural) were prevailed upon by my clever British agent to purchase a "new" Anthony novel— and that was *Steppe*. They took it in 1975, published it in 1976—and no one *else* wanted it. But virtue is not necessarily unrewarded. I was pleased with this publisher, so I shunted much stronger material to it: the CLUSTER series. The publisher loved it, published it, and resold it for paperback publication for over £3000 per volume, which was more than I had been paid by the American publisher. Then they stiffed me on my share, and that ended my relationship with that hardcover outfit.

But when they made the deal for CLUSTER they also required the paperback publisher to take *Steppe,* thus getting this loser off their hands. I understand it went for a nominal fee of £100, or under one-thirtieth of the amount commanded by the others. It was published in paperback in 1980, and also appeared in German translation that year. So *Steppe* was in print, but was not any phenomenal success.

Meanwhile, Tom Doherty of TOR BOOKS read one of the British editions of *Steppe* and liked it very much, but perceived no American edition. That was a peculiar situation for an American (actually, an American-naturalized former British) writer. Realizing that the volume had either gone out of print in America or (was it possible?) had never been published in America, he set out in pursuit of it. After all, if this interesting novel was actually begging for an American market, he just happened to have a rather persuasive contact with a prospective publisher.

His lonely quest took him along obscure bypaths, where other Anthony novels languished in Small-Press or Out-of-Print, so he bought these (after all, might as well do *something* while you're in the boondocks) and kept looking. By the time he finally caught up to *Steppe,* he had bought a total of ten Anthony books. This got my attention. I did some touching-up on one of them, *But What of Earth?,* that turned Tom Doherty's hair a shade grayer. He hurried to Florida, where we met and conversed, and TOR became a serious market for my newer work. Because my new science fiction goes to one publisher, and my new fantasy to another, and I do not break faith with publishers (or anyone else), this meant my projects in other genres, such as Horror or Historical. As it happens, I have been chafing for some time to get into such other genres, but had been balked by, you guessed it, the indifference of publishers, as the publishing history of *Steppe* demonstrates. So I am satisfied, and in due course there will be material such as has not been seen before from Anthony. And it seems that it all started with *Steppe*—the novel that no one but Tom Doherty really wanted.

Now at last *Steppe* is seeing American print, and you readers will signify your verdict on its merit by buying copies. If the novel sells well, vindicating my judgment in writing it and Mr. Doherty's in publishing it, we shall be pleased, and the likelihood is great that I will proceed to write the sequels I had had in mind at the outset, to cover in similar fashion other segments of human history. (I don't count sequels as "new"; they are continuations of the original work, and go to the publisher of that work. A prolific writer has to make some fairly fine distinctions at times.) Perhaps *Northland,* in the period of the Vikings, or *Desert,* in the time of the Egyptian pyramids, or *Sea,* as in the peoples of the Mediterranean, such as the Romans. That sort of thing. The whole world beckons, from ancient Africa to ancient America. If *Steppe* flops, then we shall be displeased, and will not inflict any more of this history upon you. Thus the readers, knowing the true nature of this series, will have the final decision. That's very fair, don't you think?

—Piers Anthony